"Luca," Polly said slowly. **"I'm not afraid of you. I'm afraid of how powerful this feeling is between us. I want you."**

The sound he made was like a growl. It made her feel electrified. "I want you," he whispered, so close to her now that she was dizzy with the scent of him. "Naked."

"Yes," she said.

They had never even kissed. But she didn't need to test her desire for him that way. She already knew.

He took her hand, and she was stunned by how rough it was. How strong. Hot. He pulled her away from the dance floor, straight through the ballroom. Her heart was racing, her whole body on high alert.

She wasn't going to regret this.

This felt like her compensation. Her severance. Her parting gift.

To finally have something from him.

To finally have some of his control.

Millie Adams has always loved books. She considers herself a mix of Anne Shirley (loquacious but charming and willing to break a slate over a boy's head if need be) and Charlotte Doyle (a lady at heart but with the spirit to become a mutineer should the occasion arise). Millie lives in a small house on the edge of the woods, which she finds allows her to escape in the way she loves best—in the pages of a book. She loves intense alpha heroes and the women who dare to go toe-to-toe with them (or break a slate over their heads).

Books by Millie Adams

Harlequin Presents

His Secretly Pregnant Cinderella
The Billionaire's Baby Negotiation
A Vow to Set the Virgin Free
The Forbidden Bride He Stole

The Kings of California

The Scandal Behind the Italian's Wedding
Stealing the Promised Princess
Crowning His Innocent Assistant
The Only King to Claim Her

From Destitute to Diamonds

The Billionaire's Accidental Legacy
The Christmas the Greek Claimed Her

The Diamond Club

Greek's Forbidden Temptation

Visit the Author Profile page
at Harlequin.com for more titles.

HER IMPOSSIBLE BOSS'S BABY

MILLIE ADAMS

PRESENTS

Harlequin® PRESENTS™

Recycling programs for this product may not exist in your area.

ISBN-13: 978-1-335-93907-4

Her Impossible Boss's Baby

Copyright © 2024 by Millie Adams

For questions and comments about the quality of this book, please contact us at CustomerService@Harlequin.com.

TM and ® are trademarks of Harlequin Enterprises ULC.

Harlequin Enterprises ULC
22 Adelaide St. West, 41st Floor
Toronto, Ontario M5H 4E3, Canada
www.Harlequin.com

Printed in Lithuania

MIX
Paper | Supporting responsible forestry
FSC® C021394

HER IMPOSSIBLE
BOSS'S BABY

CHAPTER ONE

HER BOSS REALLY was the *worst* boss in the entire world. Polly knew she couldn't prove that scientifically. But she felt like her two a.m. summons to the lair of His Beastliness was empirical evidence that Luca Salvatore was indeed the worst.

Worst, worst, worst.

She let the word serve as the lyrics for her ragey walk through the lobby of Luca's building. The night doorman didn't even ask.

"*Buongiorno*, Miss Prescott."

"Hello, Antonio," she said as she carried on through the glossy building, because there was no call to be rude to Antonio just because she hated Luca.

She was granted instant access, probably because Luca would be a bear if he was kept waiting for over two seconds. It made her want to walk slower. But then he would just make up the minutes later in the most annoying way possible. She knew it. Because she knew him.

Four years, eight months, three weeks, five days and three hours. That was how long she'd had this job. That was how long she'd been dealing with Luca Salvatore.

Dr. Luca Salvatore. Who was in fact a doctor in more than one way, because he was so obsessive and meticulous that in order to work in the innovative field of medical technology he'd gotten an MD as well as a PhD.

He was brilliant. No one could contest that.

He was also a first-class pain in the ass.

But this job had come to her in a stroke of luck so random and fortuitous the idea of walking away from it had—until this week—been completely out of the question.

For her part, she had run away from home as soon as she was able. She had gotten accepted to a university in Italy that allowed American students to study for free, and she had left Indiana faster than you could say Hoosier. She had never intended to go back home.

Not to her father's uncontrolled cruelty, or her mother's manipulations. Between the two of them, her entire life had been a guessing game. Not knowing who they would be at any given time.

They had been a nice enough suburban family by all accounts. Except for the accounts that were coming from inside the house.

She knew just how much a person could hide about who they really were.

She'd never wanted to be vulnerable, because vulnerabilities could be manipulated. She'd built an impenetrable fortress around herself using the knowledge she'd gotten watching her parents play games with each other and with her.

She'd vowed never to hurt anyone with her behavior, but she'd also made sure to take the lessons of her childhood on board and make them work for her instead of against her.

She had made sure when she arrived in Italy that she didn't look lost or confused. She had done her very best to look as if she had been to all the beautiful places thousands of times before. She knew it didn't benefit her to look open and vulnerable.

But that was how she had met people at school. Made friends. It was how she had maneuvered her way into an internship at Salvatore Medical Technologies. She wasn't specifically interested in technology, but in the inner workings of a company that size. She was studying marketing because she was so interested in how façades work. And what was marketing if not a carefully crafted and directed façade?

She was an expert with those.

She was also an expert at sizing people up instantly. In her household growing up it had been a matter of emotional survival. She could read a change in a person's mood in a moment. She didn't want to give her parents credit for her success, but she definitely felt like her ability to read a person and a moment had gotten her far.

She'd taken the lump of coal she'd been born into and made it a diamond.

She could still remember the first day at Salvatore. But only vaguely. The day she could remember with absolute clarity, was the first time she had seen Luca Salvatore.

When he had walked into the stunning, modern

building, he'd had the look of a shark cutting ruthlessly through the water. His black suit was tailored exquisitely. Showing off broad shoulders and his lean waist. He was tall, well over six feet. But it was not only his physique and height that differentiated him from every other human being in his vicinity. His face was that of a fallen angel. His black hair was pushed off his forehead, not one strand daring to defy him.

His jaw was square, chiseled as if from stone. His cheekbones hollow, his nose angular and proud, befitting of a Roman emperor.

His eyes were nearly black, and even though he didn't look at her, she'd had the sense that if he did, it would slice her neatly in two.

And then there was his mouth.

She had never given much thought to the shape of a man's mouth. But his was mesmerizing. Firm and uncompromising, and her first, immediate thought was what it might take to get him to smile.

She was, after all, expert at managing the moods of others.

She'd always had to be.

She found she wanted to manage his.

It had been an instant crush. Swift and painful.

She had never felt such an immediate attraction to another person in her life. But then, she had never seen another human being as beautiful as Luca Salvatore.

Of course, what she had discovered very quickly after that was that his personality did a lot to balance out those looks.

He was the most difficult man she had ever known.

Not the most frightening. No. Luca wasn't the type to go around hurting people. That would imply intent.

No, the thing about Luca was that he lived in his own sphere. And in that sphere the only thing that mattered was his goal.

He did not believe in pleasantries, he did not believe in compromise.

She had watched him cut a swath of terror through his staff with his willingness to fire people at will, and his near impossible standards.

That was how she had ended up with her job.

She had been standing next to his assistant—the third one he'd gone through in that month—when he had fired the other woman.

Polly had never seen a person look both relieved and devastated at the same time. Until she had come to work at Salvatore. Then it was an expression she saw often.

And when the woman turned to walk quickly out of the building, she had definitely looked both.

Upset because she had lost her job, relieved because it meant she would never have to deal with Luca again.

And then, for the first time, Luca had looked at Polly.

She had been right. It had been like being cleaved in two.

Even knowing what she did about him, what an ogre he was, how difficult he was, she had been immobilized by his beauty. Those dark brows had been locked together, his irritation written in every line of his face. She had been frightened, for a moment, that she was about to be on the receiving end of his philosophical sword. That she was about to be the next casualty of his mood.

She knew, in that moment, that she could easily be… ruined by him. That he could take her life and bend it around his with ease.

And she would always have to be on guard for that.

"What is your name?"

"Polly. Polly Prescott."

He had looked at her. As if he was scanning her. A machine taking a diagnostic of an object.

"Do you have any experience acting as an assistant?"

"Yes. I'm an intern. I assist whoever needs it."

"Brilliant. You're hired."

"I'm what?"

"Polly Prescott, you're now my assistant."

"I have school."

He had laughed.

"I will make whatever arrangements necessary for you to continue with your studies and integrate the hands-on experience that you're getting at the company."

That was her first experience with just how far Luca was willing to go to get his way.

There was no end to how far.

Her employment contract had been—and remained— one of the most ridiculous things she had ever seen. She wasn't simply a full-time employee, she was on call. Twenty-four hours a day, seven days a week. Which was how she found herself storming into Luca's building at midnight. It wasn't even a strange occurrence.

She entered the code in the lift that would take her upstairs to Luca's penthouse.

She was long past being impressed by the beauty of the place.

If only the same could be said of the man.

He made her heart stop beating every time. Made her breath catch in her throat. And she saw him for extended periods of time every single day. It was still like that.

The good news about Luca was that he was so incredibly difficult to deal with that there was no romanticizing her feelings for him.

The truth was, she was in lust with him. An inconvenience, but hardly fatal.

Sure, it consumed her every waking hour, as did he, but she was aware of it. So that made it…fine.

And possibly not even her problem soon enough.

On a whim she had applied for a job in marketing at a major Milan fashion house two weeks prior. She had been shocked when they'd called her. But they had found out that she had been an assistant to Luca for the past five years and had been intrigued. From there she'd had three phone interviews, and that morning, she had gotten the call that the job was hers if she wanted it.

She was an intriguing prospect, but more than that, she had been Luca Salvatore's personal assistant for longer than any other person had ever managed to keep the position. Luca was famous.

The breakthroughs his company had made in nano-technology for medical use were extraordinary. And it wasn't just a team that Luca had hired to make these breakthroughs. Many of them had come from him personally.

He was a genius. There was no question.

He was also renowned the world over for being one of the most difficult bastards on the planet.

That was the cost of brilliance, she supposed. When she was being charitable.

Tonight she didn't feel all that charitable.

Tonight, she had a new job offer. Doing something she actually wanted to do, instead of just being Luca Salvatore's girl Friday. Or whatever she was.

She was practically his nanny. That was the truth of it. She was in charge of running interference between him and all of the people who needed to deal with him on a daily basis. There were some days when he just simply couldn't raise his head and be bothered to spare a civil word for people he was supposed to have meetings with, and often, it was her job to go in his stead and do the communicating.

She was in charge of procuring his food, his clothing, making sure that his hotel room was exactly as he would require it. She often went ahead of him to major events and made preparations for his lodging. She managed a massive team of people, and Luca only ever had to deal with her.

It was, he had explained many times, the only way that he could concentrate on his important work.

To minimize and streamline the unimportant details.

Her job was fashioned entirely of unimportant details.

And yet she also knew that those so-called unimportant details had to be managed with precision, or her mad genius of a boss would fly into the kind of rage that nobody wanted to deal with.

She let out a long breath, steeling herself, when the elevator reached the top floor.

And the doors opened, and she stepped into Luca's pristine antechamber before using her key card to unlock the door.

She stepped inside. "I'm here, Luca."

She had called him Dr. Salvatore initially. He was quite anal about that. But she had been given permission to call him Luca three weeks into the job.

It had been strange.

It still was.

Because it humanized him.

And nothing about him was human.

"I'm in my room."

She could tell by his voice that he was in a mood. But then, if he called at midnight, he was always in a mood. He kept the strangest hours of anyone she had ever known. Sometimes she wondered if he slept at all. The truth was, he probably plugged himself into the wall for a couple of hours at the end of every day.

Maybe took off his head for a few minutes and stuck it on a charger.

She strode through his massive living area, her shoes

clicking on the black marble tile. And went straight into his bedroom.

He emerged from his walk-in closet just as she did. Wearing nothing but a pair of black pants, resting low on his hips.

He was the robot, but when she saw him her brain short-circuited.

Those broad shoulders, equally broad chest. His well-defined pectoral muscles, his abs…

If she touched him, she would probably find that he was made of steel, rather than flesh and bone. But she had never touched him, so the temptation to do so remained.

After all this time, being in his bedroom shouldn't signify. Seeing him shirtless shouldn't signify, and yet it did.

There was something obscenely sexual about his chest hair. She couldn't get over it.

He was ten years older than her. And her boss.

If she ever confessed her fixation with him to a medical professional she would be clinically diagnosed with daddy issues. But no matter how many times she told herself that she couldn't stop the fixation.

Regrettably, she had learned that for her a sexual fixation was a near impossible thing to exorcise when the object of said fixation was in her path continually.

"What are you doing?" she asked.

"I need to pick a suit. For tomorrow night's speech."

"You have to do it now?"

"Yes," he said, as if she was the foolish one. "I need

to practice the speech. And everything needs to be as it will be tomorrow."

"You can't practice in the venue right at this very moment."

"Everything needs to be the same with me," he said.

She felt the last straw descend upon her, and crack her patience completely in half. It had been a monstrous workload in the lead-up to the Singapore conference and Luca had been worse than usual. She'd been toying with taking another job as things got more and more hectic. But she'd been...torn.

Because Luca was...she'd been right. When he'd looked at her the first time she'd known he could destroy her and in many ways she'd let him. Her life revolved around him. Her every move, her every breath.

She'd thought about leaving but she had also felt paralyzed by the thought of a life without him.

Now though...

She could see herself far too clearly.

She'd told herself it was lust. She'd told herself she was armed against all things thanks to her dysfunctional childhood, and in reality she'd...

She'd been holding herself back because of him. Not taking new jobs, not realizing her own potential because she'd let herself get obsessed with him.

Or worse.

Her chest hurt when she looked at him and what was *that* emotion exactly?

She didn't want to know.

She could see he was exasperated, he didn't like having to explain himself. He also didn't care if she was tired. He didn't care if she was upset.

He cared about himself.

She'd put herself in the exact position she'd promised she never would.

Luca wasn't manipulative, not in the slightest. In that way he was nothing like her parents. But the core issue was the same. She cared for someone who didn't care for her. She bent and twisted her life to suit someone else's needs when she'd sworn never to do that.

And if she took a step back and tried to be somewhat sympathetic to the gorgeous billionaire who always got his way, she could appreciate that it must be frustrating to him to try and explain the way that his brain functioned to mere mortals who couldn't even understand what nanotechnology was, much less how it functioned in a medical setting.

She found she had difficulty drumming up sympathy for him, though.

And the truth was, she didn't need to. Because she had another job offer. What was she doing standing in her boss's bedroom in the middle of the night while he stood there shirtless, demanding an opinion on which black suit he was going to wear to speak to a room full of people?

She wasn't afraid of him. She never had been. He had said many times it was one of the things that he appreciated about her.

She met his complete, uncompromising, blunt nature with relentless cheer. Sometimes with sharpness, but always with efficiency. She had learned that half the problem he had with his past assistants was that they simply crumpled beneath the pressure of working for him. He had appreciated her backbone.

She doubted he would appreciate it now.

"Luca, I cannot believe that you called me out here in the middle of the night to help you choose a suit so that you could rehearse the speech."

"Why? It is entirely consistent with everything you know about me."

The problem was, she couldn't even argue with him.

She was going to anyway, though. "But surely you must understand that it's unreasonable."

"It is part of your employment contract. You're on call."

"Be that as it may, no normal employer would ever subject an employee to this."

"At what point have I ever pretended as if I was a normal employer? No one else is like me. You know this."

"No one else is like you," she said, looking up at the gilded ceiling in his bedroom. "I sure as hell hope so, Luca, because I don't think the world could withstand having another human being on its surface that behaved the way that you do."

"Honesty is appreciated, attitude is unnecessary."

"Oh, I'm sorry. I am running on two hours of sleep because you got me up at two in the morning after staying at the office with you until midnight. I was finally about to go to sleep and then you call me to come down to your personal residence, where you are half-naked, asking for help with something that is simply not pressing by the standards of any other human being. You are a robot, Luca. And I have tirelessly put up with you for the last five years. And I'm not doing it anymore."

"What are you talking about?"

It was all abundantly clear now. She was at a crossroads. She'd been tempted to just stay on the beaten path. To just keep on going. To just stay with Luca and stay stagnant. His favorite piece of office equipment, rather than pursuing her own dreams.

Her own life.

She had to put a stop to it.

She had to be her own best advocate because what was the point of anything that had happened in her whole life up to this point if she failed herself now?

"I quit."

"You must be joking. Nobody quits."

"No. You fire them. Because you find fault with everything they do, and I'm the one person you couldn't find fault with. But I find fault with you. I quit. I'm done. I'm going home and I'm going to bed."

"You cannot quit," he said.

"It's too bad. I am quitting. I have another job, and I don't need yours. I'm getting into marketing. I'm not going to be your sprightly little gofer, running to and fro doing whatever you want."

He looked incensed. Outraged. She had never seen precisely that look on his face before. She had seen him inconvenienced. She had definitely seen him angry. But this was something else. "We have a massive exhibition happening in Singapore next week."

"I am aware. I have planned nearly every detail of the exhibition because I'm the one that's had contact with every presenter, every person involved at the venue, everyone managing food, lodging—"

"You cannot quit before the exhibition."

"I can. And I will."

"You will not. You will give me two weeks' notice as your contract dictates."

The exhibition was all he cared about. Not her upset. Not what he'd done. And she found it sparked a fury she couldn't quell.

"You and your contract can go to hell."

She turned around. And she was just about to walk triumphantly out of the room. Finally. She ignored the tugging in her chest, she ignored the feeling of being bound to him. She ignored the pang of regret that she was never going to see Luca in person ever again, and she was just about to crow her victory, her freedom, when he spoke again.

"If you do not give your proper two weeks' notice, I will ensure that you never work anywhere else ever again."

She turned around. "I already have a job."

"*Cara*, if you think that I do not have the power to remove you from that position before you even begin, then these last five years have been for nothing. Because you have never truly known me. Two weeks. Or your professional life is over before it even begins."

CHAPTER TWO

Rage was a red haze over his vision. A sliver of ice in his gut. Worse, because it was Polly that had made him angry. And that was not Polly's purpose.

She was his assistant. Efficient, perfect in every way. Polly Prescott fascinated him, as no woman ever had.

She had been nineteen when he had first given her the job. And her innocence and inexperience in all things had been visible in those wide blue eyes every time she had looked at him.

He could never understand why other people treated her like she was older. Perhaps more experienced. It was apparent to him that she was fresh off of whatever plane she had arrived on, likely from a small town, having never been in a major city in her life.

But she was hungry. And it was that hunger that had made her such a valuable assistant. She also lacked fear.

He wanted things done exactly as he wanted them done. More than that, he needed it. He did not allow for mistakes. He did not coddle the emotions of others. She seemed to understand that instinctively.

She managed everything in his personal life that required managing. And she did so with ease. At this point, she did so without him even having to ask. The idea of having to train somebody else to do what Polly did on instinct was unthinkable. Particularly this close to the Medical Technology Summit, and to the unveiling of all of his upcoming research that was entering clinical trial stage.

His mother had been the only person in his life who understood him. Who loved him as he was. When she was gone, he'd lost everything. He'd nearly lost himself.

Where his mother had accepted him, his father had sought to change him. To fix him.

He'd always been a person who had obsessions and hyperfocus. His mother had fostered that. She'd helped him learn everything about a topic he found interesting, had added toy cars to his collection whenever possible, along with facts about different engines, makes and models.

His father had hated it. He'd thought it a sign of a weak mind to be so tunnel-visioned when it came to interests. He'd thought it embarrassing that Luca had no friends at school. His mother had told him that people who did not fit in were destined to change the shape of the world, to make it better fit more people.

He'd liked that. When he felt himself not fit, he'd imagined the shape of everything changing around him and he had felt better.

He had been a source of tension between his parents, and he knew it.

When he was nine his mother got sick. Diagnosed

with a late-stage cancer that had no hope of being cured. She'd been ignored by her doctors when she'd brought her symptoms to them, and when the illness was discovered it had been too late.

It had destroyed his life. Until he'd found a new focus.

A new purpose.

Medicine.

When it came to illness, particularly the illnesses of women, the medical community had been complacent for too long in his opinion. He had set out to learn everything he could. About technology and about the human body. About how they could both help each other.

There had been so many breakthroughs over the years. But still not the one that he had been hoping for.

But now he was on the verge of finding exactly what he needed for early detection of ovarian cancer with simple, accurate technology that would provide much more information than a blood test followed by a scan. With this, it was possible that the disease could be detected at stage one, and be screened for as part of yearly physicals.

It was the kind of technology that would have kept his own mother alive.

And while all of these things would sell themselves, and backers and researchers would be drawn to the mere rumor of its existence, he knew that making new medical technology ubiquitous was more complicated than that.

Hence the summit.

But for the summit, he needed Polly.

Whatever happened after that, he could focus on it then.

But he would do everything in his power to keep her with him now.

That was all that mattered.

"That is an incredibly horrendous thing to say to someone who has worked for you faithfully for five years."

"Quitting on the verge of something this important to someone you have worked for for five years is an incredibly irresponsible thing to do. And frankly, I thought you were better than that."

"I'm past the point of being able to be guilted into doing your bidding, Luca. I have done nothing less than everything you have asked these past years."

"And why was this the straw that broke the camel's back?"

"Because the camel had somewhere else to go. You have been unreasonable, inflexible, ogreish, some might say, every day these past five years. But I knew that it was the best place for me to be in order to gain experience for what I wanted to do later."

"And I will be an invaluable reference for the rest of your working life if you simply do what I ask now."

Yes. He was inflexible. He was in his very nature, down to his core. A person could not do the level of research that he did and also be the kind of person who bent with the breeze.

His work required focus. It required single-mindedness. It required a certain amount of selfishness around each and every endeavor.

Lucky for him, he had always been accomplished at those things.

His own father had found him confounding. Frustrating. He could admit that he had been a difficult child. Never content. Always obsessed, and there was a point where his father had been forced to contend with him on his own, and it had not gone well.

Luca could be philosophical about that.

Even if he did enjoy that his success was something his father benefited from, and therefore could not ignore. Especially as his father had told him once that he would never amount to anything, because no one as truly strange as his son was could ever make his way in the world.

So Luca had made his way in the world. And then some. Not only that, he was working to change the world. And it was precisely the characteristics his father had told him would preclude him from success that had brought him success.

Luca had found that he could pay people to handle what did not serve him or his work, and that was sufficient.

He didn't need to change. He simply needed to be powerful enough to change the world around him.

He had done so.

He did not accept critiques regarding his personality. Because his personality was irrelevant.

"Have I asked you to do anything that was not explicitly outlined as a possibility in your contract?"

"Your contract did not say that I might be called to

your home to consult with you when you were bare-chested, no."

"You seem perturbed by that."

She looked at him, and he saw her cheeks turn a slight shade of rose. She was affected by his nudity, and that was a terrible thing for him to observe. She was his assistant. She was out of bounds in that way. He had placed her there the moment he had first noticed that she was beautiful. He had not noticed immediately.

When he had hired her his immediate thought had been simply replacing one incompetent person with the next, as he knew the churn would continue.

But Polly had broken the cycle. She had become a one-woman management team. The Swiss Army knife of personal assistants.

And then one night, May twenty-fourth, four years prior, he could recall it clearly, the light in his office had caught strands of gold in her hair, as she had leaned in to hand him his espresso. It was three in the morning, and they were at the office late, with her assisting with whatever he needed.

He had been gripped then, with a hunger that had surpassed anything he had ever known before.

Sex was an appetite, like any other. He could forget about it sometimes, the same as he forgot to eat when he was deeply involved in a project. But eventually, it had to be satisfied. That was how he had always seen it.

A practicality. A necessity.

And because he saw it that way, it made it simple for him to observe the rules around it. And one very clear rule was that one did not make sexual advances to those who were subordinate.

Polly was his subordinate, and an extremely important one. Which meant that that momentary, violent hunger had to be locked away. Which he had done.

Very few things had the will to defy him. But Polly did. And in that, he supposed it shouldn't be such a surprise that on occasion the strength of his need for her defied his rules as well.

But it was nothing he would ever act on.

This was the first time he had looked at her and realized she felt the same.

She always seemed bright-eyed, efficient and practical. He had acknowledged his attraction to her, but he had never thought about her own attractions, desires. He had never taken the step to thinking of her as a set being.

She was a tool. A lovely one. But had never been a whole person to him. Why should she be? It was not reasonable or practical.

And there she was, blushing prettily and demanding that he consider her feelings around the work that he asked her to do. The schedule he asked her to keep.

"You will continue to do your job. There will be no argument about it."

"Two weeks," she said, her blue eyes flashing. The color in her face intensified, and this, he thought, was anger. "I will give you two weeks, Luca. And not a day more. That means the day after the summit ends, I'm coming back to Italy, and I will not see you again."

"I assume that means you'll be flying commercial, then. How nice for you."

She laughed. "I've survived it before. I can surely survive it again."

"I'm not certain that you can. I think that you have forgotten everything that I've given to you, because you're so dedicated to your own fiction. We both know that you are not a sophisticate. Not the one that you pretend to be. When I met you, you had absolutely no job experience."

"I was getting an education."

"And a fine one you got. But don't forget that *many* people have degrees, and the thing that sets you apart is your very particular job experience."

She looked outraged by that. Because he was right. He knew that. "Currently, what sets me apart is that my boss is unreasonable."

"What boss would allow an employee to simply walk away from something this major?"

As far as his personal story went, he was not inclined to share it with the world. That his mother had died of cancer was a basic truth, anyone could discover it for themselves if they wished. But he didn't speak of it.

It would be apparent to that person that the work he did came from personal experience. He did not know if Polly knew that. And he had no inclination to tell her.

It shouldn't make a difference.

"That's the thing. Mostly, it's not about being allowed to do anything. Because it is generally understood that a boss does not own his employee. But you treat me like you do."

"I remind you again of the contract—"

"That's all I am to you, isn't it? I'm a contract. And what you ask doesn't have to be reasonable or human. It simply has to be in the contract. You don't care at all why I might want to leave."

"You said yourself. You have no desire to be an assistant forever."

"I don't. But most especially, Luca, I have no desire to be *your* assistant forever."

He smiled. He couldn't help himself. "Is that supposed to wound me, Polly? Do you think you're the first person to remark that I'm difficult? That I am unpleasant? I know that. I don't care. What I care about is that I accomplish the work that I have set out to accomplish. I don't want friends. I don't want a wife. I don't want children. I want none of the things that would require I managed to find the sort of personality that makes other people comfortable. What I want is to save lives. That is what I do. If within that realm you find me unfeeling, then I must accept it."

She looked conflicted. But she did not argue. "You have your two weeks. But don't expect me to be cheerful about it."

"I don't require your cheer, *cara*. I simply require your compliance."

CHAPTER THREE

THE NEXT WEEK at work was a study in willpower. Luckily, Polly was in ample possession of willpower. But it was almost like Luca was going out of his way to be difficult. She would have thought that if it was anybody else. That he was doing his level best to make everything as unpleasant as possible to punish her for daring to leave him.

But Luca didn't do things simply for the sake of them, and she could say that she'd never once witnessed him being *petty*. It just wasn't him. He was a man who did things as and only when they were strictly necessary. At least, they had to be necessary in *his* mind.

The trouble for Luca was that what seemed necessary to him did not always seem necessary to other people.

Her included.

Hence the blowup over his midnight suit selection.

But where another person might have gone out of his way to be tirelessly accommodating to make her think that she had made a mistake, or would have gone out of their way to make the last week miserable, Luca was simply Luca. But in the lead-up to the summit, he was more of himself than he often was, which was a particular sort of difficult that really should almost be categorized as its own thing.

The Luca Salvatore Effect.

Perhaps she could get medical studies done on her brain after she finished with the job. Maybe it would become an officially recognized condition.

What happened to a person when they were subject to Luca over long periods of time.

If it became a recognized medical condition Luca might actually care about it, and learn about it. Perhaps that was the path to personal growth for him.

That made her smile. She suppressed it.

She was run ragged. She was absolutely resolved in her decision to leave.

She was fantasizing about the new job. About the freedom she would have there. The freedom to work normal hours. Or maybe just slightly extended hours rather than being on call twenty-four hours a day.

The freedom to leave her job and not think about her boss.

Constantly. Continually. Every moment of every day.

Even now, she wasn't in the office, she was at her own apartment making phone calls and working on the details with the hotel in Singapore, and she was thinking about Luca.

About getting his room ready when they arrived in Singapore, about exactly what he would need. About how his mood would turn even more rigid upon arrival because he would be anticipating giving a speech, being out of his element, the necessary evil of stepping away from his research.

Of course, it was to talk about his research. So there was every chance he would glory in that.

Then, her thoughts turned to how he had looked the night she had quit. His bare chest. And the anger in his eyes.

It was a confusing combination of things, things that continued to occupy her brain space in spite of herself.

But that was the problem. This wasn't just a job. There were too many things tied up in it. It had been a matter of survival. Realizing her dreams, and then eventually it had been…her attachment to Luca.

That was the problem. He was the *worst*. She acknowledged that. She knew it. She felt it. He was unreasonable. He did things that no normal person would ever do, and he expected her to do things that no sane human being would expect their employees to do. And yet, she found herself anticipating him. She found herself in some ways feeling even strangely protective of him and his eccentricities.

Then there was the fact that he was really effing hot. Which kept her from imprinting on any other man. So here she was, suspended between a raft of uncomfortable feelings, none of which she wanted.

He had been her whole life for these last five years.

Perhaps that was the problem. There was nothing and no one else. She had been far too focused on changing her life. On making something better for herself. And that had encouraged her to make her job all-encompassing. Really, the issue was her desperation. To escape what she had been. To never have to go back to the life that she had lived with her parents.

To maintain control.

In the strangest way, even though Luca was a tyrant, she *was* in control in this life. She managed all the particulars of his daily life. While she was often creating an environment that suited him, she knew everything about it.

She was the cruise director.

Perhaps that was her problem now. She was on the cusp of a change. Nobody wanted change. Change, even when it was change that you wanted, even when it was change that felt inevitable, was frightening.

She was going to move away from Rome. It had been her home these last five years.

Her first time out of the United States, and she simply didn't miss it. She hadn't gone back. She had spent these past years traveling, but she'd had this as her home base.

She had lived in the same apartment now for three years.

That was the problem.

She was leaving everything that she knew now. That was why it all felt unsettled.

It wasn't Luca.

Because she didn't want to believe that she had *softer* feelings for Luca.

When he was just the most unreasonable human being on the planet.

And yet.

He didn't care about her. The fact that his activities hadn't in any way changed in the past week indicated that. He was nothing in response to her leaving. He had been perturbed when he had first heard about it because it was a change he wasn't in control of. And when it came to not liking change Luca was a champion.

But it had nothing to do with her. Nothing to do with actually wanting her around, or caring about her in any regard.

And the same went for her.

She didn't care about him. She just felt attached to her life.

Understandable.

That was all.

When it was finally time for them to leave for the summit, she felt like there was a guillotine about to fall.

Because this was it. The end of the road.

Maybe she should have arranged to stay over in Singapore for a while after. A little bit of time between the end of one job and the beginning of another. Time to explore a part of the world she hadn't seen before, and perhaps embrace new experiences.

For one fleeting moment she imagined what it would be like if she cut loose entirely. If she forgot herself. If she found a man—a man that wasn't Luca—and had a wild fling.

Her whole being rejected that instantly.

That just wasn't her.

She wasn't a virgin out of any sense of principle.

It was only that…

You are preoccupied by him.

Was that really the only reason?

Because yes, he was sexy. Gorgeous in a way that no other man had ever been to her, but she didn't have feelings for him. Surely impossible attraction wasn't so strong that it could be the sole reason she had never taken a lover.

She pushed that out of her mind deliberately, because she knew that Luca was going to arrive any moment.

She was bustling around on the private plane making sure that everything was in order.

Making sure his favorite food and drink were available, and that everything was the exact right temperature.

"I don't see three notebooks," she said, digging around the space.

The stewardess frowned. "Aren't there two?"

"Dr. Salvatore has requested there be *three*. That is standard for any flight exceeding three hours."

"Can't he bring his own?"

She felt her hackles rising. "Dr. Salvatore does not pay a staff to ready things for him so that he can spend precious thinking time pondering the quantity of his own notebooks."

And there it was. As easy to find as ever. The umbrage that she felt on his behalf when things were not exactly as he had dictated they be.

The issue was…she hadn't done this job all these years without undergoing a certain level of indoctrination where Luca was concerned.

The man was curing cancer. It sort of balanced out the whole being an asshole thing.

That didn't mean she could or should work for him forever, but it wasn't as if she could prove his eccentricities weren't merited.

The woman looked askance at Polly and Polly felt… *peeled*. Like the flight attendant was seeing something other than Polly's professionalism at work and Polly did not like it.

"You must be new," Polly said, pinning the other woman beneath her most pointed gaze and clinging to her haughty PA front because it was better than being *seen*.

At that exact moment she heard heavy footsteps behind her, and she turned to see Luca standing there. She couldn't explain the physical reaction she had to the sight of him.

She had seen him yesterday, after all. He ought to be commonplace in every way.

But then, hadn't she just spent the past week trying to untangle why her feelings for him, her feelings about leaving, didn't seem as straightforward as they should.

"There is an issue with the notebooks," Polly said slowly. "But it will be remedied."

His gaze never left her.

"Good," he said.

Polly dialed the private airline concierge at the airport. "I need a notebook brought to Dr. Salvatore's plane within the next fifteen minutes. Yes." She gave the specifications, and then got off the phone. Because there were measurements, materials and page space requirements.

"Everything will be in place," she said.

He nodded once, and then disappeared into the bedroom at the back of the plane, closing the door behind him.

She let out a breath, and the stewardess looked at her. "Are you afraid of him? Is that why you're so concerned about his notebooks?"

Afraid? This woman thought...Polly was afraid?

She frowned. "I'm not *afraid* of him. But Dr. Salvatore is a genius. And there are certain things that he requires so that his brain is free to think about medical mysteries. I might be leaving my job but—"

"So, you don't like it. *Or* him."

This was now some weird battle of wills between her and this other woman. Like she was bound and determined to make Polly admit that Luca was unreasonable. And Polly thought he *was* in many respects, but she had context for him. And dammit she would not say it to this other woman.

"If you take issue with Dr. Salvatore and how he works, then perhaps this should be your first and last flight for him," she bit out.

Luca chose that moment to come out of the bedroom. "There is no need to be defensive of me, Polly. Though it is appreciated. I didn't realize you were so concerned with my image. Having said that, I don't care if the attendant finds me unreasonable or not." His focus was turned to the other woman. "All it requires is that she do her job. Is that possible?"

The flight attendant nodded, looking the kind of intimidated that Polly simply didn't feel around him anymore.

After all that, the notebook finally arrived, and they were able to settle in to take off.

She tried to live that experience through the eyes of a woman who had never encountered Luca before.

She tried to dissect her own response to it.

It was unreasonable to feel like Luca needed three notebooks. Luca felt like he needed three notebooks, but she knew that it was… It was one of his particular habits.

One of his ways.

She wondered when she had become so understanding to those ways.

She would like to think that she *wasn't*. She would like to think that this was just her, doing her job as well as she'd always done to the end. After all, she had just gotten angry with him about calling her to his apartment at midnight. But was that the ridiculousness of the request, the hour, or the way it had made her feel to look at him half-naked?

You don't have to know. Because you're getting a new job.

She felt relief. For the first time in a week. Maybe for the first time in five years. She didn't have to know the answer to the question about Luca. Because she simply wasn't going to be part of his life anymore.

*You were never part of his life. You might as well be
a paperweight.*

A paperweight he really liked, but a paperweight all
the same.

She had gotten very used to flying by private jet. She
liked it. It was going to be hard to give up.

But she didn't need luxury.

She wanted to be important. A main character in her
own life. She had never been that growing up. She had
been the supporting character to her parents, and she
was simply tired of it. She'd been a prop. Used when
convenient, ignored when not. They were the main cast,
they were all that mattered.

It was the same with Luca.

Because he could see one perspective, one way of
being, and it was his own. Everything else was one of
those insignificant extras.

They didn't speak, as was customary on a long flight.
She had brought a book, and Luca filled each notebook. She wondered sometimes if he did it because he
had asked for them, and he was trying to prove to himself and others that his eccentricities were a necessity.
Or perhaps he simply knew that a long flight produced
three notebooks' worth of thoughts.

"You could digitize your notes," she pointed out.

She didn't know why she said it. She was only bait-
ing him. And after hours of sitting across from him,
having food, having a nap, it was like commentary was
just begging to be made. Even though she knew better.

"I do not see the point in changing something that works," he responded, without looking up at her.

"You have endless stacks of notebooks," she said.

"Yes. I do. I also have the space to organize them."

"If they were digitized they would be searchable."

He looked up at her like she had sprouted a second head. "I remember what is in every notebook."

There was something earnest in the way that he responded to that, and it reminded her why it was sometimes easy to defend him, to feel confusion about him. He wasn't actually being difficult, or obstinate for the sake of it. He genuinely *couldn't* understand why she would suggest such a thing because he couldn't imagine having a hard time remembering where he'd written what.

She had to wonder what a childhood with a brain like that must've been like. Were people in awe of him even then?

"Have you always been like this?" she asked, saying it out loud in spite of herself.

But why not? She was leaving.

"Like what?"

"You're so particular. About *everything*. And certain. Though, your certainty is usually founded."

"You've worked with me for five years, you only now wonder?"

"I'm leaving. Maybe that's what made me wonder."

There was a clock ticking on this, she realized. She would never understand herself or what her life had been for the past five years if she couldn't understand him. It suddenly felt imperative.

"I don't know how to answer the question. I have always been myself. Have you always had your average capacity for memory?"

"Yes," she said. "I have always been this way."

"So have I. Though not always interested in medicine. My mother died when I was ten. That changed the course of my life."

He said it matter-of-factly, but there was something underlying his tone. An intensity that she recognized. It came up with certain medical discoveries. Certain things.

"I'm sorry," she said. She had never really thought about Luca's parents. She had always thought he had sprung fully formed from the ground a full-grown man.

It was impossible to imagine him as a child.

And now she was imagining him as a child in pain.

"I decided that I wanted to find out what could be done. To prevent other people dying in the way that she did. I wanted to fix it. Of course, you cannot fix something like that. Not with all the medical discoveries in the world. I might be able to prevent other people from dying, but I cannot bring her back. It is an obvious thing. But one I did not fully think of as a child. I was driven, I think to try and restore what I'd lost." He lifted a shoulder. "Now I'm simply driven."

She knew many of his other employees thought of him as emotionless. But she'd always known that wasn't true. He had a great many emotions surrounding what he wanted and needed in his environment. He could be exacting, short-tempered and ill-humored. All of which were emotions.

What she hadn't witnessed were…softer emotions.

But now she was forced to imagine him as a small boy. Missing his mother. Believing, on some level, that he could use his incredible brain to bring her back.

"What did you…think about before then?" she asked.

"Toy cars," he said.

"Toy cars?"

"*All* cars. But I had a large collection of toys."

"Did your parents buy them for you?"

"My mother did. My father thought it was strange. To collect something so obsessively and know all of the details about it." His lips curved upward. Almost a smile and yet somehow not. "It is strange. He was correct."

She felt bound up by the sympathy blooming inside of her. Looking at his stark, handsome face as he recounted loss, pain.

The feeling of being different. An outsider.

She knew that all too well. She'd always felt outside. She hadn't been able to invite friends to her house because her parents had been so volatile and unpredictable. She'd made a mask of ease that she wore with the outside world. She'd learned to fashion herself into a very nice facsimile of someone who was having a normal experience of life and growing up. She'd learned to close herself off, to protect herself from her mother's fractious insults and her father's explosions of verbal rage where he'd been willing to say anything, no matter how cruel, to get a response.

Like reducing the people around him to tears was the ultimate source of power.

She'd become a placid shell. Watching, always taking in information from the scene around her, never ever giving the deep, real parts of herself away because that would mean exposing herself to pain.

She'd thought it would arm her against Luca, she supposed. But the problem was, he wasn't manipulative.

Luca could only ever be Luca.

It was…him. And perhaps it was that lack of veneer that had finally gotten beneath her protections.

"I don't think it's so strange," she said softly. "And anyway, why would you make your child feel like they were strange?"

"He didn't want me to be. He was quite a successful man, my father. Relatively, I mean. He wanted me to be like him. But in order to do that, he felt that I would need to behave differently. He was a salesman. Everything he did was about connections. I was bad at them. But, I found success my own way. I don't need to learn the things that he thought were so important. I simply need to lean into my own strengths." He looked down at his notebooks, and then back at her. "That does mean filling in three physical notebooks on a long-haul flight."

She sighed. "I suppose I can't argue with you."

"You could," he pointed out.

She could, but it would be like flailing at a brick wall.

"I don't need to," she said.

She decided to take another nap. And by the time they landed, she was well-rested.

A car met them at the jet and whisked them away, and she did her best not to marinate on the conversation they'd had earlier. Did her best to not sink into sentimentality.

Why had she ever asked him these things about his life before? She could imagine him, a small boy, left with the one parent that didn't understand him, and it made her chest get tight.

Of course, now Luca was a genius billionaire, so when people didn't understand him they mostly said nothing.

But it was still a function of his life. A feature of who he was.

It was still a thing he had to cope with.

He was a terrible boss. He was inflexible, and completely one-track-minded. And yet, he was nothing like her parents. And perhaps that was why, in spite of herself, she felt affection for him. Or something adjacent to affection.

The realization made her heart jump, and she began to catalog the details around them. The beautiful buildings, the pristine cleanliness that was normally absent in major cities.

It was genuinely one of the most spectacular places she had ever seen in her life, natural splendor colliding with man-made innovations.

She could see why he had chosen this place as the

site where they would learn about new advancements in medicine.

This place felt like the future. Luca was brilliant when it came to anything that had to do with his work.

And something else entirely when it came to other details about life.

But he was honest. And there were no guessing games with him.

Maybe that was why she wasn't afraid of him. Maybe it was why she didn't find him intimidating in the way that many people did.

Because she would rather know where she stood. Even if the ground was precarious.

When they arrived at the hotel she was momentarily distracted by the glory of it. Traveling with Luca meant she had been exposed to a heavy amount of luxury over the past few years, but this was beyond her expectations.

The hotel was a square column with great open sections that spanned several floors, held up by lit pillars covered in twining vines. A resplendent representation of nature in the middle of the city.

The lobby was modern and sleek, with a great glass pillar at the center, almost like a greenhouse, containing a veritable jungle while all around them were modern amenities and clean lines.

Luca barely gave their surroundings a second glance. Instead he went directly to his room and left Polly to see to the details. Both of the summit itself and their star.

She didn't mind. This would help her get out of her own head.

Because there was no time to think. Everything was moving at a rapid pace. She had to ensure that all of the details were in order.

These sorts of events were the part of her job she loved the most.

There was a certain amount of smoothing over his interpersonal relations that she did, and she enjoyed that.

She realized that she was Luca's marketer in many ways.

She sold the man, because he refused to do it.

His work sold itself, but he… He was another matter.

When she checked the clock she realized it was nearly time for the opening speech of the summit.

Of course, Luca would be giving it.

He was a very compelling public speaker. For all that he lacked when he was trying to make connections around the room, he compensated for it beautifully when he was on the stage. He was such a magnetic man. So brilliantly handsome. So absolutely enthralling.

Maybe she was biased.

She didn't think she was.

Until this past week she had been convinced she didn't much care for him at all, but faced with the prospect of leaving him, her thoughts were turning in an entirely different direction.

She used her key card—because she always had a key to his room—and let herself in.

And was stunned when he walked out of the bathroom wearing nothing but a towel slung low around his hips. Water droplets were sliding down his broad, well-muscled chest, and she felt desire strike her like an arrow straight between her thighs.

Why was she doomed to encounter him half-dressed so many times in a row? It wasn't like it had never happened before, but it hadn't happened quite so frequently.

"I'm sorry," she said.

She felt her face betraying her. It was so hot she knew it had to be bright red. Surely he wouldn't miss that.

"It is no matter," he said, as if he'd missed it entirely.

For all he seemed obsessed wholly with his work, she knew he had lovers. His lovers were part of what she dealt with on occasion when he was too busy to manage them. Once he was done with them, he was done.

And yet, he always seemed so dispassionate to her.

It was impossible to imagine what it would be like when he was with a woman. When he...

Perhaps, virgins should not attempt to fantasize about how their bosses made love.

Made love.

There was no question that Luca did not make love.

He would probably be the first to say it. In wholly blunt terms.

She couldn't even hate him for that.

He was honest. And maybe that deserved some level of appreciation.

It wasn't his honesty she was appreciative of at the moment, however.

"It isn't professional," she said.

"Right," he said.

For a moment he looked apologetic. And she realized he had thought that she meant him, and not her.

"I meant *me*," she said. "I should have knocked."

"You have a key to my room for a reason. You are supposed to assist without interruption."

"Still. It would have perhaps been a good idea for me to make sure that you were not in a state of undress."

"I am not a maiden," he said.

She looked at him. "Was that a joke, Luca?"

"Yes and no. It's true. But also, I was being funny."

She laughed, in spite of herself. Because every moment of the last five years hadn't been terrible. And this one certainly wasn't.

"Well. It was amusing."

She felt a sudden tension rise between them, and she turned away from him. "I am going to get ready. And I will meet you in the ballroom."

"As you wish."

CHAPTER FOUR

LUCA COULDN'T GET Polly's expression out of his head. She had been looking at his body. It wasn't the first time. She had done so at his apartment last week the night she had quit.

She was aware of him physically. And she was nearly not his assistant anymore, which was pushing the bonds of his control.

He could not want her.

And yet.

He liked clear rules, and he liked to follow them. He spent so much of his time pondering the mysteries of humanity. Of science. The human body, and what men could accomplish when they studied that body.

There was no room for gray areas in his life.

Polly had been his first window into understanding the lure of reaching for something you should not touch.

Obsession, he'd called it. Because he was familiar enough with obsession and that didn't have to be sexual. It wasn't forbidden for him to catalog her outfits, her mannerisms, the way her hair moved when she tossed her head. And how it changed depending on whether she was amused, annoyed, or upset.

Obsession, because it could be nothing more.

Or rather, it had never been able to be more because she was his assistant and he would never, ever violate his position of power by seducing his assistant.

He thought about how she was leaving him, and he was beset by rage again.

But there was something about the rage that stoked the fire of that forbidden desire even higher.

This was not attraction as he knew it.

He was attracted to women. Their round bodies, their softness. He was not particular about the particular shape or features of a woman. He simply enjoyed the all-encompassing air of femininity. Soft skin, floral scents. When he indulged himself, he appreciated every aspect of that indulgence.

But it was never *this*. This aching pull that he had felt ever since that night last week.

Her defense of him on the plane had added a strange sort of sensation to the mix.

He was also not a man who enjoyed novelty.

He liked to be assured of things. To be certain in them.

In his work, he dealt in the miraculous and mysterious. He did not need any more of it. That was what he told himself. And yet, he found himself being fascinated by her in new and distracting ways.

And he was not a man given to distraction.

"Go and ready yourself," he said.

She nodded, and scurried from the room, as efficient as ever.

And he was left to get ready. Everything he was meant to wear was chosen, and ordered, so that it would be easy for him to put together, easy for him to find which suits went with which speech.

It was no matter to him whether anyone understood that or not, but for him, each detail flowed into one another. And it was an exceptionally important thing. Disrupt one link in the chain and the whole of it was compromised.

He would have to find someone else who could handle his details.

He thought of that as he put on his black shirt, black tie and black suit. He did not have to run through his speech again, he had it memorized. Each and every word. Every pause.

He was very good with this sort of thing. He had ample time to rehearse. If he could rehearse everything, he wouldn't need an assistant. But unfortunately, life moved at a pace, and interaction was often random.

None of that mattered tonight, though. Because tonight, he was going to be giving the most defining speech of his career, introducing the early detection processes and technologies that had been so long missing from the world of medicine.

Everyone wanted a cure for cancer. He among them.

But in the absence of a cure for advanced cancers, early detection was almost as good.

He would be saying just that tonight.

There was a knock on the door. He knew that it was her. She did not normally knock, but she had indicated that she thought she should have after walking in on him in a state of undress. Also, it was just how she would knock. Brisk, efficient. Not timid, even though what had occurred earlier had clearly embarrassed her.

He was fascinated by his assistant. He had made a study of her.

How could he not?

He had never known anyone like her.

She was expert with all people. Soft when she needed to be, hard when it was required. She seemed to possess the ability to make anyone feel at ease. And the truth was, if he could see that it must be profound.

She also seemed to take people exactly as they were, with no questions. She evaluated them and the situation, clearly and cleanly, and then moved on.

She accepted him in a way no one else ever had.

Not since his mother.

"Come in," he said.

The door opened. And there was Polly, wearing a fuchsia-colored dress that conformed to her curves, hugging her body tightly, flaring out down past her knees. The neckline was plunging, revealing the plump curve of her breasts.

Damn, but she was beautiful. He was not a man who wanted what he couldn't have, as a general rule.

That had been a choice.

It had nothing to do with compartmentalizing or appetites or anything of the like.

No. It had to do with being a small boy who looked at groups of kids playing together and couldn't figure out how to approach them. It had to do with loving a mother who had gone, never to return.

Having a father he could never please no matter how hard he tried.

He had given up on desiring what he could not have.

He was a billionaire. There was never a reason—not one—for him to ever be desirous of that which could not be his.

And yet, he wanted her.

In that moment, more than he could remember wanting anything.

It was a craving.

What would it look like, peeling that dress away from her body, exposing more of her skin?

He nearly growled, but he held it back, because he knew well enough to know she would find that disturbing.

"It suits you," he said, keeping his tone brisk.

She blinked. "Thank you."

"Everyone in attendance will be very impressed."

"With your assistant?"

Polly was occasionally miscaptioned as his date. It never bothered them.

He didn't bring dates to things like this. There was no reason. He didn't need to date, he needed somebody who understood him. Somebody who understood the business.

Someone who could take what he was trying to say and spin it into something interesting.

She was very good at that.

He did not take her arm, he never did, though he had known a momentary temptation to do so.

They walked out of the hotel room together, and to the elevator.

She was beautiful at his side, as ever. And he found himself fighting the urge to touch her.

He was on the cusp of the most important thing he had yet discovered and launched to the public, and he was drowning in novelty. He didn't like novelty.

He could not afford the distraction. This was not the launch of a product designed to simply generate income. This was something that could very well change the world. His libido had no space in the equation.

He was a man of infinite control. In fact, it had never even been difficult for him.

One fuchsia dress and a pleasing collection of rounded curves would not derail him now.

They moved into the ballroom, all the glittering opulence. He felt the tension sometimes, the necessary generation of massive funds when it came to working with this sort of technology. He wanted everything to be freely accessible to those who needed it. And yet, the actual work itself required massive amounts of money to keep it moving. And so, it required playing a game. It required the generation of wealth.

His own personal fortune had been amassed with investments elsewhere. Property portfolios, and other work. While his medical corporation generated billions, it was all put back into research, and medical funding.

For him, the act of making money was a simple thing. It all related to that focus.

Focus that would not be splintered now.

He moved away from Polly and made his way to the front of the room. His very presence signaled that it was time for everyone to take their seats.

And then, he took his place on the stage. Every word, every inflection was planned. And every portion of the speech was articulated exactly as he had intended.

He knew exactly what he was about.

The excitement in the room was palpable. This discovery changed so many things.

And while the room was full of a great many investors, people who cared primarily about the monetary value of something like this, there were also people who took it for what it was.

A chance to save lives.

And the truth was, while the medical-industrial complex certainly had its issues, issues that Luca himself fought against, it was also made up of people. And even investors loved people who got cancer. Even they felt an investment in this change.

Because the truth was, they lived in a world where money could only help with your treatments to a point. If the ability to discover and detect an illness didn't exist, then you were not insulated. Not even by your billions.

Everyone benefited from this.

"As part of the research phase, we will be looking specifically at monitoring those with family history who cannot pay for conventional medical care."

A ripple went through the crowd. "We will be sourcing participants from around the world. That way we can see the effectiveness on people who come from a variety of backgrounds. It is important to our research that we spread the information as broadly as we possibly can. We must collect all the data that we can. This is the beginning to what we truly all hope for. A cure. And this proves that we are not defeated by answers that have eluded us for all this time. There are still discoveries to make. And we will make them. This is the beginning of a very exciting summit. We will pool knowledge, and together we will find the answers to the most pressing medical concerns we face in society."

The applause when he got off the stage was deafening.

He ignored it. He didn't do this for accolades.

They were immaterial.

He did not do this for glory.

He felt Polly's gaze on him, he knew it was her without having to look.

But he did look, and he saw that her eyes were glistening.

She was emotional. He wondered why.

It was not, after all, a personal thing to her, at least not as far as he knew. He had done a background check on her when he had made her his assistant, and nothing in her files suggested she had experience with losing a family member to disease.

He went to his table, one occupied by the chief investors, and sat by Polly. He ignored the investors and leaned toward her. "Are you upset?"

She shook her head. "I'm not upset. I'm simply moved. I understand more now why this matters to you."

She cared about that? She was angry with him. If she wasn't, she wouldn't have quit.

It made no sense that she would be moved to tears by his experience in that case.

She changed the conversation, shifted it, included the investors. She was good at that. She maneuvered it so that he had only to answer questions about the research. And peppered things with delightful, humorous anecdotes and personal remarks. The kind of conversation that left everyone feeling as if they had had a good interaction with him, even though Polly had done most of the conversing.

He did not know what he would do without her.

Anger began to build inside of him, and it only got worse in the following days. As she continued to prove utterly indispensable, and ravishingly beautiful every night for the formal events.

What had been contained by the rules of society, of professionalism, now felt less clear. He'd banked his need for her all this time because it was the right thing to do. But she was leaving now, which meant every word, every interaction, felt like it had a different meaning to it. Different rules.

Or worse: no rules at all.

He was a man who often relied on rules.

And now she was Polly, without the fence of appropriate boss/employee relations surrounding her.

So when she did something for him, he couldn't simply dismiss it as her doing her job.

When he earned a smile it no longer felt like it was strictly her duty.

When her fingertips brushed his he wasn't obliged to pretend he didn't feel sparks of electricity winding through him, that his gut wasn't tight with need. That his body wasn't on high alert.

It built, over the course of all these days. It was nearly physical pain.

The hotel itself was one of the most storied venues in all of Singapore, and yet Polly made it look pale in comparison.

It was such an odd thing. Her beauty had always been undeniable. And yet, she had never been the type to actively court attention. Her beauty had never been *sensual*.

It was as if it was a costume that she put on, and yet once he had seen the inherent sensuality in her he could not unsee it.

He felt utterly entranced by it. By her.

On the last night, she wore gold. She was utterly resplendent, and he was meant to focus on the conclusions of the week. All upcoming research projects from universities and smaller medical tech companies. He was choosing investments himself, that he might help further broader medical research.

That should be his focus.

And yet, he found himself captured by Polly. He noticed that many men were. Her long hair fell in waves over her shoulders. Her body was on tempting display, barely covered by the liquid gold gown she wore.

And after this, she would be leaving his life forever. It was the thing he had been avoiding thinking about. Suddenly, it was all he could think of. It filled his mind, filled his vision.

She had been everything these past few years. She had been compelling, constant, consistent.

She was the content of the inner workings of his life. And he could not remember a time when he did not have her.

At the same time, he wanted to bury his fingers in her hair and claim that sweet mouth for himself.

He thought that, standing right in the glittering ballroom where everyone was celebrating a successful summit.

He thought only of kissing Polly.

What if he did? What if he claimed the one thing he should not have? What if he claimed the one thing he should not want? How different would it feel?

Perhaps he could do something with this gnawing ache. This craving, by making it real.

Suddenly, sex became something different. Something beyond the usual appetite, something beyond even a general craving.

He would die if he did not have her. He was not a man given to excess. And so this first experience of wanting something excessively was like a drug.

He had never taken those either. Only because he knew himself to be a man of obsession. A man who would likely lose himself entirely if addiction were to ever meet obsession.

And yet, that was what she felt like.

Addiction. Obsession.

Something he could not control.

People were dancing. He never partook in such things. These were nothing more than business events to him, and he did not participate in the more festive aspects. But as he saw her standing there on the edge of the dance floor looking on, he realized that either she would stand there alone—which was a crime all on its own—or another man would ask her to dance. Another man would take her in his arms.

He could not allow that. He crossed the room to her. "Luca—"

"Dance with me," he commanded.

"What?"

"You do not need me to repeat myself. You heard me. Dance with me." He realized then that he had repeated himself anyway.

"Oh."

That was neither an affirmation nor a rejection. So, he took her hand without waiting for either one. He brought her out to the dance floor and pulled her against his chest. The contact was electric. Her breasts brushed against him, and he wanted nothing more than to clear the room and strip her body of that offending dress. It was beautiful, and yet it was an obstacle. And he supported the removal of obstacles.

"Luca," she said, her eyes round. Was she afraid of him? Or was it something else? He could not read it. He did best when emotions were simple. Like science. When there were definitive answers. When things became open-ended he found he could not know them, and when he could not know something, he was only ever angry at it. And yet, he was not angry at her.

"Do I scare you?"

"Yes," she whispered.

"I'm sorry."

He stepped away from her, regret filling him.

But she took a step toward him, and put her hand on his forearm. "No, Luca. You scare me because I want you too."

CHAPTER FIVE

HER HEART WAS thundering in her ears. Had she really just told her boss that she wanted him?

Had she really just *assumed* that he wanted her?

But the way that he had touched her...

Luca was a great many things, but subtle was not one of them. And the last week had felt like an assault. Like suddenly all that was sensual in him had been turned on to her, with the full force of a tractor beam.

It had been the most exciting, delicious, terrifying week of her life.

She had done her best to ignore it. But every moment of every day had only ramped up her arousal. Had only made her desire more insistent.

She was leaving him.

He was the only man that she had ever wanted like this.

She was sure every therapist in the world would say that that was not how you dealt with your daddy issues. She didn't care. She didn't want healthy. She wanted something that felt good. She wanted something for herself.

Because her feelings for Luca were a complicated tangle and she was never going to be able to work through them.

She was taking another job. She was moving across the country. She wanted him in a way that blotted out any potential need for other men.

She wanted him.

It was a terrible thing. A great and terrible thing.

"Be explicitly clear in what you mean," he said, closing the distance between them. They were surrounded by people.

Everyone would know.

But then, the fire that had burned in Luca's dark eyes these past few days had been bright enough, hot enough for anyone to see it.

In fact, one of the female scientists had said something to her just last night.

"I thought he was your boss. I didn't realize the two of you..."

"We aren't."

"He certainly wants to."

"It would be inappropriate," she had replied.

"Sometimes inappropriate is the most fun."

She didn't think she wanted Luca because it was *inappropriate*. Rather she wanted him because...

Because she had never known anyone else like him. Because she had never seen a man so beautiful and remote. He was like a lost gem, and he would hate to be compared to a gem but it was true. He was hard, all angles and brilliant light.

He was painful to look at. Painful to care about.

She did care about him. That was the worst part.

How could you not care about a man this brilliant? This singular?

And it had never been easy. It had never been anything half so simple as having a crush on her boss.

She knew every inch of Luca's life. Every brick that comprised who he was. And she knew that there was not a single space for another person. Not as a partner. Not as anything other than a useful tool.

But she knew also that this was the only way that she could ever purge that need for him.

Now that she actually would be leaving him.

The very idea of trying to love Luca made her want to die. A woman could dash herself upon those rocks over and over again, and she would never find any satisfaction.

She had seen women leave his home.

Looking high on the experience of having been with him. He never called them again.

She knew because eventually she had to block or reroute their calls. Luca wasn't a playboy, but he wasn't celibate either.

He had told her once, very bluntly, that for him sexual release was a necessary function. But that he felt nothing emotional about it. Any more than he would eating a meal.

That lived inside of her.

And the same likely couldn't be said for her. It was

very possible that if she slept with him she would experience emotional ramifications. And he wouldn't.

But she was strong. She could withstand it.

And tonight, she was finally going to get something that she wanted out of this relationship. Maybe for a few minutes, he would even see her as a human being, and not simply a more complex than average paperweight.

What would happen if she was honest with him? If she told him this thing was destroying her from the inside? That it was growing so unbearable it was part of why she was finally leaving, this sensation that she cared for him while she was nothing at all but furniture to him? That it felt too big to be contained anymore?

That she didn't understand it. Because how could she when she'd never even touched another man?

She wasn't going to admit that.

"Luca," she said slowly. "I'm not afraid of you. I'm afraid of how powerful this feeling is between us. I want you."

The sound he made was like a growl. It made her feel electrified. "I want you," he whispered, so close to her now that she was dizzy with the scent of him. "Naked."

"Yes," she said.

"What is the protocol? Do we have to stay? Will we be seen as rude?"

He was genuinely asking. This was part of her job. Guiding him when the social situation didn't make sense to him. Though he didn't often ask so bluntly.

The truth was they would be seen as two people sneaking off to have sex. Which was exactly what they were.

"Everyone will know," she said. "They won't find it rude. Though we might end up being the subject of gossip."

"I don't care about that," he said.

"Neither do I."

She was leaving. She wouldn't be part of this world anymore. She didn't care.

They had never even kissed. But she didn't need to test her need for him that way. She already knew.

He took her hand, and she was stunned by how rough it was. How strong. Hot. "Then if they already know, there is no reason to be subtle about it."

He sounded relieved by that. He would be. He wasn't subtle. Thank God. Because another man might not have answered her so honestly regarding their shared desire. There were no games here, and for a woman without experience, that was ideal.

He pulled her away from the dance floor, straight through the ballroom. Her heart was racing, her whole body on high alert.

She wasn't going to regret this.

This felt like her compensation. Her severance. Her parting gift.

To finally have something from him.

To finally have some of his control.

Oh, she'd dreamed of it. As much as she'd tried to pretend she didn't. As much as she'd told herself she wasn't unendingly curious about how he was in bed, she had wondered.

Did he ever let himself off leash entirely?

And what was that like?

All that focus, force and obsession, zeroed in on another person.

The idea was dizzying.

They were silent in the elevator, and then, his hand over hers, he led her back down the hall toward his suite.

He opened the door, and closed it. And as soon as it closed behind them, he wrapped his arm around her waist and pulled her heart up against him. Her breath exited her body in a gust.

Right then she wanted to cry. Right then it was too much, and so was he.

She was leaving him. He was infuriating. Why wasn't it simpler?

"Do you know how much I wish I could hate you?" she whispered, their mouths a mere whisper from each other.

"Why is that, *cara*?"

"Because you're the worst boss. Because you don't see me as a human being. Because you have treated me like an incidental these past five years."

"I treat you the same way I do everybody else."

The words were a knife's blade, turning inside her.

"Exactly," she said. "And you shouldn't. You should treat me like I'm special. Because I do things for you that nobody else does. And now I know for sure, you feel things for me that you don't feel for anyone else who works for you."

"It is attraction, Polly."

He said it so blandly. As if it could never be that simple.

"Nonetheless, Luca, the way you treat me leaves me feeling so hungry for something more. You make me so angry, you make me feel small sometimes. And yet I can't hate you. Because you are the most complex, interesting man I have ever known, and do you have any idea how much it pains me to say that? A man shouldn't be interesting and complex simply because he displays baffling behaviors."

"I am baffling even to you?"

"Yes."

"I thought you understood."

He almost sounded hurt. If he had been anyone else she would've imagined that he was. Perhaps that should make her feel bad. But it didn't. "I baffle you and yet you want me anyway?" he asked.

"Yes," she said. "And I feel like I deserve this."

"You are so confident you will enjoy it?"

"Aren't you?"

He moved closer, and she felt like she might faint. Being this close to all that beauty had left her feeling nearly drunk.

"No more talking." The words were hard. Blunt. Arousing.

That was when she found herself crushed roughly against him. His mouth crashed down upon hers, and there was nothing left to say. There were no more words left in her entire being. She was made entirely of need.

His mouth was hot and hard, his tongue insistent as a requested entry. She granted it. She wanted him to devour her. She wanted…

This was such an explosive fantasy. Seeing him like this. When he pulled away from her, he was breathing hard, his eyes wild.

She had done that to him.

It was different than his frustration over his exacting standards not being met.

This was him at the edge of control. This was him pushed to his limit, by her.

She had power.

And she felt electric with it.

She had never been kissed before. And yet she was confident that no kiss could ever match what his did.

Because he was the man who had changed her life with a glance. She had been so certain she had seen him, and evaluated him as she did everyone. That she had seen everything. But nothing could have really prepared her for him. It was why he was dangerous and wonderful all at the same time.

And now that she was leaving, now that this was it…

She could finally have him. Just for tonight.

This explosive, wonderful, terrible, dangerous, sharp thing.

She was confident that no one could ever fully understand what this was. It wouldn't be like anything else that had ever existed before or since.

Luca Salvatore was a singular man.

She knew sex with him would be singular as well.

As if determined to prove her point he wrapped his arm around her waist and lifted her up off the ground as if she weighed nothing. He carried her through the sitting room, propelled her back into his bedroom.

"I want to see you naked," he said. "Do you have any idea how much?"

There was something burning in his eyes that was completely unfamiliar to her. She had thought that she had known Luca and all of his moods. But here it was. The hidden depths. The thing that she had never seen. She had imagined that he might be during sex as he was with everything else. There was an intensity to him, yes. But it was always entirely within his control.

He seemed to be pushing at the bonds of it now.

There was…desperation in his eyes. She had never imagined that. It took her breath away.

"No," she said. "Tell me how much."

She needed it. After all these years of feeling like nothing more than a particularly useful paperweight to him, she needed to hear that it was different. Now, at the end of this. At the end of them, she needed to hear it.

"I know everything about you," he said. "About the way that you move, about the way that you complete tasks. There is a very particular way that you hold your wrist when you are annoyed with me. A way that you move your head when something interests you. You smile a particular way when you are pleased, and a different way when you're upset. I don't normally notice those sorts of things about people, but you have been an object of my fascination from the moment I first hired you. You are a study in contradictions. I think most people don't notice them, but I do."

She wanted to hide. She had never imagined that Luca looked at her that way. She had never imagined that he looked at her like much of anything.

She'd never thought, for one moment, that he had *seen* her quite so clearly.

"But…"

"You don't think I notice details like that. But I only know details that matter."

There was nothing he could've said that could've possibly aroused her more than making it clear that she mattered.

But this was somehow more than sex.

He kissed her again, hard and insistent. "I do not know how your body looks without clothes on," he said. "I'm studying your face now. Your eyes are filled with… I don't have a word for it. But you like this."

"I do," she said, not feeling embarrassed, not at all, because this was just so honest. He was honest. That she had always appreciated about him, whatever else was going on.

"I've never seen you aroused."

"You have. It's only I do a good job of hiding it, I think."

"Not always. Though I would consider you interested, not aroused in those moments. I noticed the way that you looked at my body when we were at my house."

"*Anyone* would want to look at your body."

She found it easy to return his honesty with honesty.

"Anyone would want to see yours."

"I can assure you that is not the case," she said. "But I'm glad that you do. For my purposes at the moment."

He reached behind her and grabbed the zipper of her dress, releasing it, letting the dress fall around her waist.

Need arced through her, and she found herself more aroused as her breasts were exposed to him, as the dress slipped down over her hips, revealing that she was wearing nothing more than a pair of very brief underwear.

She wasn't embarrassed. Because of his honesty. Because he made his appreciation for her form so apparent as he gazed at her.

"Beautiful," he said.

He kissed her neck, and then he bit her. She gasped. She wrapped her arms around his neck and he consumed her. She began to tear his clothes away from him. She didn't have the patience to go slow in deference to her inexperience.

She didn't have patience at all. She needed him. Like air.

This was five years in the making. Whatever she had told herself about how she felt working for him, this was undeniable.

She wanted him.

Every night she had spent in his bedroom watching him dress, every time she had been pinned beneath his stern gaze. Every time she had watched his intense anticipation when he had been working on a project, it had all coalesced into this moment. It had been foreplay.

Even if she hadn't quite appreciated the extent of it. She did now. She was slick with need for him.

She was also innocent. She didn't know what was happening to her body.

She knew all about sex.

She knew about climax.

She had brought herself to it more than once.

She was human, after all.

She was just a very guarded, protected human, which meant that always, these things had been better for her to experience on her own. Without anyone else.

She let out a shuddering breath as he kissed her again. As he moved them both to the bed, as he removed all the layers of clothing between them.

"Please," she said. "I have to see you."

He moved away from her, and she looked at his masculine form in awe. She had seen his bare chest many times. But never so that she could openly stare at it. So that she could touch him. She reached her hand out and placed it flat on his chest. "You're beautiful," she whispered.

He made a rough sound of male satisfaction. Then she let her eyes move down lower. To that thick, aggressively male part of him.

She had never seen a naked man. She was not one for sexual images, even though she didn't have an issue with people who did enjoy them.

She had just never been interested.

She had on occasion brought herself to climax at night when she couldn't control her riotous thoughts. Her fantasies about her boss.

But she didn't go out of her way to seek out sexual arousal. There had never been a point to it.

He was the first. And he was... He was beautiful.

Just as she had known he would have to be. Because he had called to her, always, in a way that no one else and nothing ever had.

If there was one thing she trusted about herself, it was her instincts. When it came to people and what they were concealing. And she had sensed that what he was concealing was something that she wanted. She had been correct.

"Have you looked your fill?" he asked.

"No," she said. Because she knew, somehow without a doubt, that this would never be enough.

"Touch me," he said, his voice hard.

She reached out and pressed her fingertips against his chest, dragged them down his stomach, all the way down to that hard, masculine place between his thighs. She wrapped her hand around his shaft, biting her lip as she did so. Experimentally, she stroked him. She thought about telling him that she was inexperienced, but ultimately changed her mind. She didn't want anything to alter the experience between them. She wanted to have him. All of him, as he would have any other woman.

He closed his eyes, his breath hissing through his teeth. And then, it was like he couldn't bear it any longer. Then, he was kissing her. Then he had her pinned to the mattress. She wrapped her arms around his neck, parted her legs for him, and he pressed that hot, hard length against her slick flesh. She groaned, arching against him. He kissed her neck, down to her breast, sucking her nipple in deep. She couldn't breathe for how glorious it was. He moved down, so that his face was between her legs. He cupped her rear and lifted her up off the mattress, devouring her most intimate heat as if it were a delicacy he couldn't get enough of.

She didn't even think to be ashamed. She didn't think to hold back. She moved her hips in time with every stroke of his tongue, every scrape of his teeth. She was lost in it. She felt like she might die. He called yet more and more desperate sounds from her body, and met them with sounds of masculine hunger.

He pushed two fingers inside her slick channel, filling her. She cried out in pain and pleasure, her internal muscles pulsing around him as an orgasm was extracted from her with the most intense precision.

It was Luca Salvatore to his core.

Even in this he was unmatched.

Even in this he was everything.

When he looked up at her, his eyes were nearly black, his pupils expanded so much he was pure predator. And she could see that he had lost all control. He moved his body up the bed, gripped her thigh and hooked it over his hip as he kissed her, as he thrust himself inside of her with one brutal stroke.

It hurt. She cried out into his mouth, but he swallowed her pain. And turned it into pleasure. He began to move, hard and unyielding, taking no quarter, taking no prisoners.

He was so deep inside of her she could scarcely

breathe. She could feel him, each dominating inch as he claimed her over and over again.

Whatever she had been before this, she couldn't remember. For now, she was simply Luca. And he was hers.

He was not her boss, and she was not his assistant.

She was not leaving.

And he was not cold.

They were together. They were a conflagration. An expression of need burning so hot, so bright, that nothing would ever be able to dampen it.

With each stroke, her pleasure built. Until she was at the end of herself. At the end of everything. She came again, a hoarse cry of need escaping her. And his own release came on a roar as he poured himself within her.

She was left storm-tossed, sweat-slicked and exhausted.

He did something entirely unexpected. He pulled her into his arms and held her fast as their breathing calmed. And then she found herself drifting off to sleep. When she woke, it was with a start. She was still lying next to Luca. They were both naked.

And she knew she had to leave. She had no other option. Because if she stayed, she would never be able to go.

She felt like she had been slashed with broken glass.

She felt like she was destroyed. And she couldn't be destroyed. She had to remake herself. That was the whole point of taking this other job. It was the whole point of leaving him in the first place. It was the whole point of taking this chance and having one passionate night with him.

She had to leave. She sneaked out of the hotel room, and he never once stirred. She went back to her room and gathered her things.

Then she went straight to the airport, and got the first flight back to Italy.

And as she sat in her economy seat and stared out the window, she tried to come to a place of acceptance with the fact that she was never going to see Luca Salvatore ever again.

CHAPTER SIX

OBSESSION WAS LUCA'S strength and weakness. It was what enabled him to put his head down and work tirelessly to find a solution to whatever problem was pressing against him in the world of medicine. It was what had delivered his success to him—both financial, and in terms of scientific discovery.

It was also what crippled him now.

He could think of nothing but her. After launching the greatest medical discovery of his career, he could not think of medicine. He could think only of Polly.

It was unacceptable. Never in his life had a woman bewitched him so. Never had a woman commanded his mind and his body in such a fashion. It should not be so. And yet it was.

He could not account for why he was so obsessed with her. It had been sex. Nothing more. It was extremely common for him to not be able to remember the physical details of his lovers after the fact. He could remember the rush of release, but not the specifics. His brain simply released them, because they were not important.

The details of Polly's body, of the way she had cried out his name, the way that she had clung to him, haunted him.

He could not forget.

He had never wanted to forget quite so much.

He cursed his brain, and the way that it was put together, which was not something he had done since he was a very small child.

He had taken all of his weaknesses and turned them into strengths. He had dominion over them. Except in this. Except with her.

It was good that she was gone. It was good that she had gone to Milan, to marketing. And he had done as he had promised. He had written the most sterling recommendation letter for any person that had ever existed. Because he was a man of his word.

He was. In spite of what she thought about him. In spite of what she had said about him seeing her only as a thing.

He fought the urge to sweep everything off of his desk. His brain was cluttered, and his surroundings were not, and yet, he found that *everything* bothered him right now. Even his notebooks.

Because of her. This was all because of her. Her breasts, her lips. Everything. The way that she cried out his name, the way that she had clung to him after.

Then she had run away.

Her audacity. She could have stayed.

Yes, he had told her that she would have to make her own way home, but clearly in the aftermath of their sexual encounter, he wouldn't have held her to that.

Clearly.

Clearly.

But then, she didn't want to feel anything for him. She thought the absolute worst of him. And perhaps he had no right to feel unhappy about that. He found that he did. He swept his notebooks onto the floor, picked up his coffee cup and threw it at the wall. It broke. The mess was not satisfying. The broken mug was not satisfying.

Nothing was Polly.

Nothing did anything to ease the ache inside of him, not even his research. If he saw her again he would...

Why leave it to chance? He should offer her her job back. Offer her twice the amount of money. He couldn't function without her. It had been eight weeks. And he was no closer to feeling like he could manage himself than he had been when she left.

Yes.

He would go to Milan and offer her her job back. He would not call. He would show up in person. And then he would be able to work out his obsession with her easily. Because she would not be a fantasy living like a ghost all around him at all times.

She would be back in her physical form. And she would be his assistant again. Which would put up a barrier.

That was the problem. The lack of rules surrounding Polly anymore meant that his mind was free to dwell on the sex. He would simply restore her as his assistant and all would be well. Yes. That's what he would do.

He had chartered his private plane for Milan only moments later.

It would take no time at all to get there.

Luca didn't even fill one notebook on the flight. Granted, it was a short flight, but the behavior was out of character. When he had attempted to write, he had only managed one word: Polly.

It was unbearable.

Unendurable.

She had taken his brain and she had done something to it. Hijacked it.

And then she had left him.

He was a mass of teeming energy by the time he disembarked from the plane. By the time he got into the waiting car to wing his way down to the fashion house.

It was across a large, crowded square, a massive historic building that stood proud and tall, and inconsequential as far as he was concerned. It was nothing compared to the work that he did. And nothing compared to the work that she could do with him. If she needed to feel more appreciated, if she needed him to learn a new way of speaking with her, then he could do so. He could learn.

He had made efforts to do so before, and he could do it with her.

He was determined in this.

He walked across the square, and he saw a door open at the top of the massive stone steps. His gaze was drawn there, to the flurry of movement, a red scarf, blond hair.

It was her.

His body recognized her on a cellular level. It was not visual. It was visceral. He felt her. To the depths of himself.

It had always been so. It wasn't just her movements that fascinated him, he realized now. It was the movement that she created within him, different than any other human being.

Different than anything.

His.

It was so clear then.

She belonged with him. Together, they would make massive advancements in medicine, and if she needed a new title, promotion, if she needed to be second-in-command of the company then she could be so.

Because she was what made him work.

He strode up the steps, without pausing, without thought.

She saw him.

She felt him. He knew it. Because he could see it there in her eyes. That recognition. The shifting of the tides within her soul, he knew it, because he felt it.

He felt what another person felt. He was confident of it.

It was a novelty.

Something he had been told he was incapable of. Something many people had said he did not possess the ability to do, and he had done it. Without even trying. Hell, he didn't even want it. But there he was, standing there, making eye contact with Polly, absolutely certain that what was happening inside of him was the same reckoning inside of her.

She shook her head. And he nodded as he approached her.

"Yes," he said. "I've come for you."

"No," she said. "You shouldn't be here."

"There is nowhere else that I ought to be. I think you know that."

"I don't know that." There was something fearful in her expression now, though in the past he knew that she had said she was afraid of him only because of the degree to which she wanted him. Maybe it was the same now, and yet he didn't think so.

He did not like that.

"I'm not here to hurt you. I'm here to offer you a job."

She blinked. "A job?"

"This past month has been hell. I cannot function without you. I need you."

"You… You need me?"

"Yes. I have tried. I have been through one assistant every week since you left. Nothing works as it should. My life is disordered, and I cannot afford to have a disordered life. I need you."

"You need me to do things for you," she said.

Yes. He did. And yet, she made it sound as if it was inconsequential. It was not. It was everything to him. His work, his life, the way that it functioned. He felt as if he was crawling out of his skin without her there. As if he was going to have to unzip the essence of what he was so that he could find release by expanding to fill the room, escaping his human form.

It was terribly uncomfortable, and something he had not experienced since…her.

"I need you to come back and work for me."

"I don't want to come back and work for you. I have a job."

"I will give you a promotion. I will double your pay."

"Double?" She looked stunned.

"Yes."

"That's outrageous and astronomical."

"It is not. I will make you second-in-command of the company if that's what you wish. I will give you shares. Whatever it is you want, but I need you back." He was on the verge of debasing himself, did she not see that?

"Luca," she said, her gaze sparkling with fractured light. "We slept together. And you have come to my place of work to tell me that you need me…to come back and do a job for you."

"Yes. I have thought of nothing else since you left."

"You have to be kidding me. I'd… I gave my virginity to you, and *you* have been thinking of nothing but how I…used to bring you coffee?"

He didn't know what to do with the first part of what she had said, so he let it filter past, and dealt with the comment about the coffee. "It is not only coffee. My notebooks are in disarray, no one has been able to anticipate—"

She howled. Like an enraged beast. "You have got to be kidding me!" She stepped away from him.

"Wait," he said. He returned back to what she had said. About her being a virgin. "I didn't know," he said. "That you had not been with anyone before."

"Well now you do."

"Why?"

"Because my boss was such a demanding, controlling pain in the ass that I never had time to go on a date, never had time to get a kiss, much less get penetrated. The hilarity is, it had to be you." She shook her head. "It had to be you because you're the only man that I know, because you…" She stared at him, her breasts rising and falling as she seemed to be grappling with what to say next. And then she simply turned away from him. "I can't do this, Luca. You're you. And I have always respected that. You are a man who is infinitely complicated. A man who is meant for bigger things than getting his own coffee. I understand that. You're trying to save the world. But I'm not. I'm just trying to save myself. I have to live. And I can't do it with you. I cannot be your assistant." She started to walk away, and he gripped her arm, stopping her, turning her to face him.

"Don't leave me," he said.

He saw all the color drain from her face, and then he noticed the circles under her eyes. That her lips were the wrong color. That her body had changed. Yes, her body had changed. She was wearing a sweater, different than the stark skirt suits that she had worn when she worked for him, but he could still see that her breasts were larger. There was a hollowed-out look to her, and yet her waist was not smaller. He frowned. "You don't look well." Terror overtook him. She looked exhausted. She looked… She could very well be a woman with the disease that he feared most. The disease that he…that he had spent his life fighting against. "You must go to a doctor."

"I'm not unwell," she said.

"Yes, you are," he said. "You look remarkably unwell, and in fact you look like…" He found himself struggling to say it, and he was a man who was nothing if not matter-of-fact.

"You don't need to worry about me," she said.

"You look as if you might have cancer," he said.

She covered her face with her hands, and he could see that she was pressing hard against her eyes. "I don't have cancer, Luca. I don't… I'm pregnant."

CHAPTER SEVEN

SHE FELT DEVASTATED. Standing there looking up at the horror on his face. She hadn't been able to let him think that she was sick. She just couldn't do it. Even after…

When she had seen him charging up the steps she had been certain that he had known somehow. How could he? She wasn't certain, but he was well-connected with the medical world, and she wouldn't put it past him to put some kind of alert on her name, privacy laws or not.

They hadn't used a condom the night that they were together, and surely he must realize that.

She hadn't thought about it until it was far too late to do anything about it. But he must have… Luca Salvatore did not forget anything. And yet, he had forgotten a condom. And she was living with the consequences of it.

Though, she had decided that she was not… She wasn't sad about those consequences.

She had been shell-shocked at first, of course. But the more she had sat with that, the more she had realized she wanted this baby. That she wanted a chance to build a real, healthy connection with her child, to love someone wholly and utterly without the need for protection. Not only that, she was more than able to take care of a child physically. She had an extremely supportive employer, she made enough money.

She knew enough not to repeat the mistakes of her parents.

And perhaps it wasn't ideal for her baby to not know its father, but she had thought that maybe someday in the future…

Except she couldn't imagine Luca as a father.

Staring at him now, at the abject horror on his face, she still couldn't.

He hadn't come for her. He had come for her excellent personal assistant skills. He had not come for the baby, he had come for his own convenience.

She hated that moment where she'd hoped it was for her. She hated herself for feeling it, for being so weak with him. Always.

She had decided that she would not be telling him about the child. Except… Except then that horrible, stricken look on his face when he had thought that she might be genuinely ill.

"You cannot be," he said.

"I assure you, I am. Medically confirmed and everything."

"No," he said. "That isn't possible. I have taken my share of lovers, and I have always exercised precautions."

"Luca," she said, outraged on so many levels right at that moment. "You didn't use a condom."

Yes, they were in fact standing on the steps of the

Milan fashion house yelling about condoms, but at least they were speaking English. So probably only three quarters of the people around them knew what they were talking about.

"Yes, I did," he said. "I never forget such things."

"You did," she said. "You did with me. You forgot, because you had a…a human moment. That's what people do, Luca. They throw away all of their good sense so that they can have an orgasm. And that's what we did. We didn't think of anything. Not the repercussions, not the consequences to each other, not the devastation that it might create. We decided that nothing else mattered except being together, and look at what it's gotten us."

He looked undone. And the thing was, she was pretty sure that he was more upset about forgetting to use a condom than he was about her being pregnant. More upset that he had been called out on overlooking something, which she was entirely certain he had never done before.

"You must come with me," he said.

"I must do no such thing. I am on my lunch break, and I intend to go eat."

"Then I will go with you."

"No," she said, beginning to walk away from him.

"You cannot stop me from walking on a public street," he said.

"I could call the police and tell them that you're harassing me."

"People know who we are," he said. "They know that we have an association."

"You're a genius, Luca. You cannot be unaware that women are often harassed by men they know. Particularly men they had slept with."

"It is not harassing you to want to know more about the situation that you find yourself in." He paused for a moment. "The situation we find ourselves in."

She let out a heavy sigh. "Oh, Luca. You don't have to do anything in response to this. I had already decided."

"Are you not keeping the baby?"

"I am," she said. "I had a difficult relationship with my parents, and I am never going to have a family if I don't make one myself. This is an opportunity for me to do that. I'm financially able. And therefore it just seems…like a reasonable time for me to have a baby. But I don't need you to be involved."

He frowned. "But I am the baby's father."

"Yes. You are. But many fathers are not involved in the day-to-day lives of their children."

"But those men are bad fathers."

"Maybe not. Not if it benefits everybody for the man to stay away."

"You think the child would be better off without me?"

He said that with so much genuine wonder that it made her feel like she had been stabbed clean through. It was easy to think that Luca couldn't be wounded. Yet it was clear she had hurt him.

It was so difficult, because the truth was, she suspected that he wouldn't be a good father because of the way that he was. Because of everything about him. Because of the way that he had to live his life. And yet she didn't want to hurt him.

She hated the revelation that she was able to *hurt* him.

Luca had always seemed invulnerable and untouchable, and today he seemed undone in a way that she didn't care for.

She especially didn't want to be the cause of it.

"Think about it," she said. "You don't want a child. You can't even handle having to get a new personal assistant. If you think your life is disordered now, think of how disordered it will be when there's a baby. You won't be able to do things whenever you want, you will be subject to the schedule of another human being. You've never even had a relationship, have you?"

He shook his head. "No. I haven't."

"And why is that?"

"It doesn't fit into my life."

"Exactly. And I knew that about you. I knew that about you when I slept with you, and I know it about you now. I never expected more from you than one night."

"You did not ask me what I wanted."

"You just said it doesn't fit into your life."

He met her gaze, his eyes like steel. "Then my life will have to change. Because it already has. Because you are pregnant with my baby, and I will not be a bad father."

"I don't know what you think—"

"You will marry me. And return to Rome with me today."

* * *

Luca's brain was working as fast as it ever had. He had to react appropriately. It had never been more important. He was a genius. He knew that. He understood the inner workings of the human body in ways that most did not. His brain was filled with an enormous amount of education, but while he understood the inner workings of the human body he often did not understand the workings of the human mind. The human soul.

It hadn't bothered him, not in general. Because he had fashioned a life that catered to his strengths and not his weaknesses. Because what he was accomplishing with the human body mattered much more than him connecting with a few other people.

He had assumed, when he had bothered to think about it at all, that this was simply the balance of things. If you could understand one, you would not be graced with understanding of the other.

But he needed both now. He needed all of it now.

Because he knew one thing for certain, he would not be shut out of his child's life. He would not have his child thinking that its father didn't want them.

That was impossible.

He knew what that felt like. He had been a motherless boy, because his mother had died. She had not chosen to be away from him, and it had been an unbearable pain.

But in many ways he had been fatherless. With the man living in the same house that he did. In many ways, he had not had a father, and that was the other man's choice.

If any one thing had devastated him in a way he could not find purpose for, it was that.

He had lost his mother, but at least in that he had found the aim of his life.

He found nothing in the rejection of his father except pain.

He could not bear the idea of being *that* for his child.

Could not bear the thought of a child walking out in the world with a wound because he had not been able to…change.

"I have a job here," she said.

"Can you do it remotely?"

"I don't know. I don't know if I want to."

He wanted to offer to move his own work, and yet he did not think that he could manage that. He was on the verge of changing many things in his life, but that felt a bridge too far.

"We can sort that out later. It does not have to be all the time. But while you are pregnant I want you near me. I want to be able to see for myself that you are okay."

"I'm going to be fine. Many, many women carry babies and give birth every year."

"And some of them die."

He had meant that to be an expression of concern. She looked at him in horror. "Luca," she said. "No pregnant woman wants to hear that."

"I've never spoken to a pregnant woman before, not as far as I know, so how would I know that?"

"Clearly. Clearly you never have."

"Marry me," he said.

"No," she said. "You ran me down in the streets of Milan to demand that I come back and work for you after we had a night together. I don't want to marry that man. I don't want to marry a man who can't even acknowledge that he forgot to use a condom with me, because he needs so desperately to maintain his control."

"I admit it then," he said. "I lost control with you. I didn't even realize that I did. Do you have any idea how terrifying that is? I have never once in my entire life done something that I wasn't fully aware of."

It galled him to admit it to her. It was something he hadn't even fully been able to admit to himself.

"I think that isn't true. I think that you have done a great many things in your life you're unaware of, it's just that you don't realize you've done them because they affect other people's feelings. And you don't care about that. You never have. Everything in your life is about you. And I... I accept that on some level, I understand it. I even... I understand why it needs to be that way. But that doesn't mean they are the kind of man I want to marry. Caring about you would be a terrible mistake. It would end only in pain."

He felt like he had been slashed about the chest. Felt like he had been physically wounded. What she had said about him was so...so desperately unflattering. So outright, plainly...true. He was everything that she said. His life was centered wholly on himself.

Hearing her say it made it seem like less a necessity of his work, of himself, and more of a flaw.

And he would have to change it, but in order to do that

he would need her to come back to Rome with him. In order to do that, he would need her to come with him. He would need his child. So he had to stay uncompromising, he had to continue to see things his way in this moment so that he could do the things that she was suggesting he try to do. At least, that's what he thought she was doing.

"You must let me," he said. "You must let me try."

"You can try by inches. You can try by coming to see me. By fostering a relationship with me that has nothing to do with the company. By...coming to visit your child after they're born."

"No," he said. "You must marry me because that is the right thing to do. Because statistically children do better when they have two parents in the home."

"Statistically, maybe, but when one of the parents is a genius billionaire, and the other one is financially solvent herself, I'm pretty sure that they might be able to defy generalized statistics."

"If you care about this baby then you must want what's best."

"Of course I want what's best. Don't forget that you found out about this baby fifteen minutes ago and I have known for a while now."

"You weren't going to tell me."

He might have gone his whole life never knowing. She had thought it would be best.

It was like a stab wound. He did not indulge his feelings. He never had. If he did...he would never get anything done. He practiced perfect control in all areas of his life because if he did not, the world would control *him*.

His father had despised him. Everything he was. Everything he thought and did. To live in that sort of environment and feel the weight of his every disapproving breath would have killed Luca. And so he had learned to close off his own sensitivities and focus on his mind, not his body or his heart.

But she had gotten to him.

Deep.

She shook her head. "I really wasn't. Because I knew that it would end... I knew that it would be this. Proclamations and demands, and forcing me to meet your expectations."

"You knew that I would want the baby, and you were going to withhold them from me?" Any guilt that he might've felt at forcing her hand now was completely mitigated by that.

"That isn't exactly..."

"You will marry me. Or I will fight you for full custody of the child."

"How dare you?" She took a step toward him, and he was almost certain she was going to strike him. "How dare you threaten me."

"It isn't a threat, it is a fact. One of us has to have primary custody of the child, you think it should be you simply because you're a woman, simply because you're the mother. I do not. I think that it should be me because I possess greater resources than you do."

"Financially, maybe, but when we are talking about

the thimble where you keep your emotions, believe me when I tell you your resources are not greater than mine."

"Do you think I'm this way because I feel nothing?" He leaned closer to her, the rage inside of him building, growing, expanding, claiming every part of him, taking control of him. "I am this way because I feel everything. And if I paused every moment of every day to ponder those feelings I would never get anything done. I would never do anything. If I felt all the things within myself, there would be no new screenings. There would be no new discoveries. I would be lying on a floor somewhere probably addled out of my mind on some substance or another trying to figure out a way to stem the tide of pain that lived within me. Do not ever tell me that I don't feel as much as other people. The air around me offends me. Why do you think I need everything managed the way that I do? I feel *everything*."

She looked shocked by that. Good. He did not speak about himself. It wasn't an interesting topic of conversation, and he wasn't friends with anybody. So there was never a reason to try and explain to another person how the world worked for him.

It had never been a reason. But there was one now.

"And if you have a child who was like me, if you have a child who cares only about toy cars, and doesn't know how to speak to other children, then what? Because I know... I know what it's like."

"It doesn't give you the right to force me into things," she said.

"The way I am doesn't give you the right to exclude me from them either. And because we are both immovable, we are at an impasse. And the one with the most power is the one that can force the bend. I have the power, *cara*. You can decide what you wish to do in response. Bend or break."

Any guilt he might've felt was stemmed by his resolve.

Her eyes filled with tears. And he did not let himself care.

"Fine. I'll marry you. Legally. I'll give you what you're asking for, but on paper only. You will… You will make me second-in-command at your company. But I will not work directly beneath you. I will work in the public relations portion."

"That is acceptable."

"I want my own wing of your house. I will not encounter you in a hallway unless I choose to."

"Done."

"That means we will not be living in your penthouse."

"I don't care. Consider it vacated."

"If you wish, you could stay there."

"I will live under the same roof as my child."

"As you wish." She looked at him, her gaze hard. "If you make this miserable, believe me when I tell you I know how to make it hard for you too. Because I grew up with parents who were extremely accomplished making each other's lives hell."

"And how will that be for the child?"

She looked as if he had struck her. "I know enough to

know how to keep it away from the child, because that is something my parents declined to do."

"Do you think they also thought they were not including you in their games?"

"Don't speak to me of games. Not when you're playing them just the same."

He shook his head. "This is not a game to me. You will be my wife. There will be no argument."

"I'm not sleeping with you."

"I didn't ask you to."

They never made it to lunch. Instead, she was bundled back on his plane, she quit her job over the phone, and they were back in Rome before dinner.

"I'm sorry, I don't have this imaginary house you imagine we will be sharing different wings of," he said. "We'll have to make do with another room in the penthouse tonight."

He gestured to the door, and then went off to his own room.

He closed himself inside, and let the silence bear down on him. Everything in his life had changed in a single day. He preferred change to take place over a very long period of time, slowly and surely, if it had to occur at all.

But he would marry Polly as soon as he could obtain a license. He would change.

For his child, he would change everything.

Because everything he was, everything he had done until this point had been a tribute to his mother. And what would any of it matter if he could not pay tribute to the flesh and blood he had created?

It would not matter at all.

And neither would he.

Polly didn't think that he would be a good father. But it didn't matter what she thought.

What mattered was what he would do.

CHAPTER EIGHT

POLLY SAT ON the edge of the bed, shell-shocked.

She had said things to Luca that she deeply regretted. Because they had been unnecessarily hurtful. She had been lashing out because she was upset. Because she was afraid. But then he had reacted… He had reacted the way that she had been certain he would. Inflexible, cruel in kind, when he didn't even mean to be.

She hadn't told him the honest truth. She hadn't thought that caring about him would be hell.

But that loving him would be.

She cared about him already. That was the problem. She had cared about him for quite some time, in spite of herself.

And now she had let him drag her back here, had quit her job…

If she had loved her job then perhaps she would have fought harder on that point.

The truth was, it was difficult to care as much about marketing for the fashion house when…she really did believe that Luca was changing the world. And she really had felt in some small part that when she was working with him, she was working in tandem to do so as well.

She believed so strongly in what he was doing.

Part of her was happy to be back working for the company, particularly in a position that suited her better.

None of her was happy about the surrounding circumstances.

She hated herself for the threat that she had issued. Was it so easy for her to decide to be like her parents when it suited her?

They had been so cruel. It had been up to her to manage their feelings, and it had been such a painful existence.

And when backed into a corner, she had been the same. Manipulative, taking things she knew to be weaknesses and exploiting that to hurt the other person.

She was deeply unhappy with herself. And yet, she was so tender regarding the whole situation that she didn't know what she could've done differently.

How could she accuse Luca of not knowing how to deal with people when she had just proven that in a difficult situation she was no better?

The question he'd asked haunted her. Would she know what to do with a child like him?

She wanted to think so. After all, she had been very good with Luca. And not in a sacrificial way. She... She had come to appreciate him. The way that he was. Except then she had been cruel. She had used that as an excuse to allow herself to not deal with the complexities of their situation. Because that was the truth of it.

She had chosen what she had thought to be the path of least resistance.

It had been cowardly.

Maybe that was why she had given in to the marriage demand. Of course, she didn't want to find herself in a situation where she didn't have custody of her child, but she had to wonder if in part she had given in as penance. Because when she had heard herself throwing her own reasoning back in his face she had been appalled.

She was appalled by him as well.

Neither of them had been the best versions of themselves.

But they had both been true to type. And even more difficult truths to stomach. He had been inflexible, and she had bent round his inflexibility to whisper poison in his ear.

She had hurt him, and so he had lashed out. She didn't want to be hurt so she had done the same.

And now she was marrying him.

If she didn't marry him, she might lose custody of her child. He was a billionaire after all.

More to the point the idea of sharing anything with Luca—especially a human being—seemed exhausting and impossible.

Maybe what you're really afraid of is living in the in between.

Maybe.

Maybe what really felt impossible was being with him without being with him.

In her ideal scenario, she didn't have to be with him at

all. It made it easier, to just ignore that he'd ever been the biggest part of her life. If she could make him disappear.

But she couldn't have that so in many ways marrying him seemed easier than...

Than living near him, seeing him, dealing with him, without actually having him.

That made her feel like she was weak but...

She might be weak right now. Just a little. She certainly wasn't cool, collected Polly who knew how to work a room, but didn't let it work her.

She felt thoroughly *worked*.

She stood up from the bed, and wiped at her eyes. She should go and apologize to him. Maybe. Except she was afraid. Afraid of what would happen if she went to his room. Afraid of what would happen if they were alone. Not because of what he would do, but because of what she would do.

He had haunted her dreams this past month.

The terrible truth was, she had missed him. Even the infuriating things about him.

It would be such a terrible thing to love him.

I feel everything...

His words scraped against a raw part of her soul. She didn't want to consider that. Didn't want to think about the possibility that he felt more than everyone else. And that was why he was the way that he was. It was easier to dismiss him when she had convinced herself he wouldn't care.

But she had been confronted with how very much he did care.

With her own callousness, and her own inability to look at another person and really see them.

How could she accuse him of that when she had done the same? How could she act like he was somehow less able to consider other people when it was clear every person did it all the time.

Everyone made themselves the main character.

She had done the same.

She lay down on her bed, and tried not to weep.

But she did anyway.

She could remember crying piteously the first time she was aware of her parents forgetting her birthday. They'd been on a high with each other and had planned a weekend trip away. She'd been left alone at nine to make her own dinner and put herself to bed.

She'd cried, and no one had been there to care.

She had never wanted to be sad and small and crying because she couldn't get what she wanted from another person, never again.

But here she was, weeping over a man as impossible as the situation she found herself in.

And she couldn't escape to Rome, because that's where he was.

She had been running for a very long time, and she had finally reached the end.

The next morning, when Polly got up, it was late, and Luca was nowhere to be found.

But it was past time for him to be at the office, so

it stood to reason that he was there. He was a creature of habit.

She maneuvered around the kitchen, which was relatively familiar to her. It was perhaps childish to demand that he buy a whole new house so that they could avoid each other. She had been angry. Furious.

They were going to have to have a talk, and she was going to have to find a way to be fair. Because she hadn't been.

She had beaten herself up about that until she had fallen asleep. She knew that she was going to have to bite back a few of the more regrettable things that had come out of her mouth.

She went to his very fancy espresso machine and made herself a coffee. Then she stood at the window, looking out at the city below. It was difficult to fully figure out how she had gotten here.

And yet, it was five years in the making.

Of ignoring feelings for him that had been building, of declining to take care of her sex drive. Yeah. That was the problem. Her latent sex drive. And not the fact that she had been wholly obsessed with Luca.

She gritted her teeth. She had heard of pregnancy hormones making women emotional, but she had never heard of pregnancy hormones forcing women to be brazenly honest with themselves. She didn't like it.

She sat down on the wide, ridiculously large couch that took up most of his living area. And when the door opened behind her, she nearly jumped out of her skin.

"Luca," she said.

"Yes," he said.

"I didn't expect you."

"Why is that?"

"I assumed that you were at work."

"Why?"

"Because that is your routine," she said.

How absurd, to sit here with him and speak to him about work. How absurd the last few days had been. They had been naked. She had tasted this man. He had been inside of her. And yet... He had come after her about the job. And then he had claimed her because she was having his baby.

And still, they weren't acknowledging the passion.

Truly, her internal honesty was getting to be a little bit much. "I was not at work," he said. "I was seeing to the business of getting our marriage license."

"What?"

"Yes. We're getting married. Now."

"Now?"

"Yes. Should you like us to wait?"

"I... I assumed that we would be having a wedding."

"It will be a wedding. Though not one that is traditional or shrouded in ceremony. Simply something legal to ensure that everything is as it ought to be."

"Oh."

She had never really given any thought to getting married. She had never thought she would get married.

She scanned herself, trying to see if she felt any sadness over not getting a fancy wedding with a wedding dress and people looking on.

No. She didn't want that anyway. Would his father come? Her parents? All of that seemed silly. And anyway, a lot like inviting pain and trauma that neither of them especially needed especially in the middle of all of this.

"It will… It will be in the news," she pointed out.

"I'm known for being practical. I don't think anyone will think anything of it. Anyway, this is not pretense. You're having my baby, we are getting married."

"People already know we… There were some items about us sneaking away during the summit. After your triumphant speech."

"Were there?"

"Do you really not read any press about yourself?"

"You know that I don't. I find myself steadfastly uninterested in anyone else's opinion of me. It does not benefit me to read, therefore I don't."

"Very admirable, Luca, but a great many people wouldn't be able to keep that up."

"I'm not other people."

She let out a hard breath. "No. You aren't. To that end, I have to tell you that I'm sorry about some of the things that I said yesterday."

"That's nice," he said.

That rankled. Was *he* not sorry?

"We both said things we didn't mean."

"I didn't."

"You… You didn't?"

"No. Not at all. I only say things that I mean, Polly, you should know this about me."

"You mean, you weren't being a less evolved version of yourself to get your way?"

"Of course I said things in order to get my way, but that doesn't mean that I didn't mean them."

"I... Never mind. I'm not sorry."

"You were quite hurtful."

"I don't care."

He shrugged. "That's fine. You're not the first person to say such things to me."

That, she found, was more bothersome than it had a right to be. That he found her basic, and like everyone else. What a horror.

"I... Let's go. Let's just get this over with."

"You are angry with me," he said.

"Well spotted."

She stood up, and just stood there for a moment. "I should change."

"You don't have to."

She was wearing a soft pair of black pants and a matching shirt. "I should."

"Because it's a wedding?"

He was wearing a suit.

"No. Because I don't want to look shabby next to you."

It was a silly thing to say, because anyone or anything would look shabby standing next to him. Luca Salvatore was nothing if not spectacular at all times.

With that in mind, she disappeared into the bedroom, and procured one of the items of clothing that he had set there. It was a soft blue dress, knitwear, and forgiving. But it was nice, and it flattered her figure, even as it changed. She put on some makeup. A bit of nude lipstick and some shiny eyeshadow. Some blush, because otherwise she was going to look like the corpse bride.

She was marrying him.

And as she walked back out to the living room and saw him standing there in that dark suit, it was like a truth rang inside her, clear and bright as a gong. It wasn't even that weird that she was marrying him. Because if she was going to marry somebody it almost had to be him.

Because Luca was the single most defining relationship of her life. He had been, even before she had slept with him. He was a man that she was singularly preoccupied with. A man unlike any other. She shouldn't want to touch him again.

It would be the worst thing in the world to love him.

She reminded herself of that. She didn't feel quite as much conviction as she had before.

"Now we can go," she said, eager to move past the moment.

She noticed that Luca's tie was crooked. Out of habit and impulse she moved forward to straighten it. But when her hands made contact with the fabric, she was far too aware of the heat emanating from his body. The scent of him. The sound of his breathing. She saw about her task, and moved away from him quickly. "There. Everything is right."

"Yes," he said, his dark eyes fathomless. "It is."

They did not touch one another as they departed from

the penthouse, and made their way down to the lobby. He opened the waiting car door for her once they got outside, but she managed to avoid his touch even then.

They were driven to a small building, historic in spite of the fact that it was nothing more than a registrar's office.

"I thought it was slightly complicated to get a marriage license in Italy."

He laughed. "Nothing is complicated when you are a billionaire. And of course we'll draw up a document to protect both of our assets."

"A prenup?"

He nodded. "Of course. It is sensible. It will hold both of us to the terms we'd agreed to."

"I suspect you already have that all handled?"

"Obviously."

She wondered right then if that was the real reason he pursued wealth. Another way to eliminate complications. He certainly didn't seem to revel in luxury.

She was marrying a billionaire.

That thought made her feel slightly off-kilter.

They were taken before the officiant, and the ceremony was done in Italian, with no fanfare whatsoever, and no kiss. It was simply a legal matter. They both signed paperwork, and she had to sign an extra paper making it clear there were no impediments to the legality or morality of her marriage.

All in all, it took no time. And she felt foolish for changing. Felt foolish for believing it would even be half so momentous as a ceremony in front of a justice of the peace. It wasn't that. It wasn't anything.

It was quintessentially Luca, she supposed. All business, nothing else. When they found themselves back in the car, though, his gaze met hers.

"You are my wife," he said.

He said it matter-of-factly, as he did many things, and yet it made her burn.

There was an answering heat in his eyes that made it difficult for her to breathe.

"And you are my husband," she said. But the moment she did, she had to purse her lips together, as if to bite off the rest of that statement.

She looked out the window, her heart beating in her chest like a trapped bird in a cage. They had agreed that this wouldn't be…physical.

She was supposed to have a job at the company. They were going to raise the baby together.

She looked at his profile, taking a chance at pinning her gaze to him again. What would it look like? Raising a baby with him? She hadn't even wrapped her head around what it would look like for her to raise a baby with herself.

She was caught up in a sweeping tide of change. One that had begun with her deciding to leave him. And had ended with her back here, married to him.

She was utterly stunned by the whole thing.

Suddenly, she felt dizzy. She had been unwell off and on the past few weeks. Not morning sickness so much as sickness whenever it felt like showing up. And it was definitely happening now.

He studied her. "You don't look well."

"I'm…fine."

What good would it do to let him know that she felt like collapsing? What good would it do to show weakness?

Her parents had only ever used it against her. He had tried to use the baby against her.

She turned over that harsh, sharp thought. What he'd done amounted to using their child as leverage, it was true. But the subtle difference was he had laid it all out on the table in front of her, rather than trying to manipulate her.

She shoved that to the side.

She wasn't angry with him, not like she had been before, but she couldn't trust him either.

She couldn't trust anybody. She never had, she was hardly going to start now not when she needed to keep her guard up the most.

She was vulnerable. More than she had ever been. She was growing a life, thank you very much.

And then she was going to have to figure out how to raise that life.

That made her falter internally. Because there were things about herself she wasn't sure she had dealt with. Things that gave her pause when it came to the idea of raising a child. Because her child would depend on her. Her child was going to be learning about life from her, and…

She suddenly felt utterly, desperately unqualified.

"What is the matter?" he asked.

"I'm overwhelmed. By the idea of raising a baby. By the fact that we're married. You can understand that, surely."

"Perhaps that's true, but I also think you're physically unwell."

The car pulled up to the front of their building, and she began to unbuckle, but he got out of the other side of the car and rounded it, opening her door before she managed to free herself. Then he bent at the waist, and reached down to pluck her up from the car like she weighed nothing.

She wasn't used to that. He had never touched her before that night in Singapore. And then, his touch had been decisive, and bracingly, unapologetically sexual.

But this was…

He was holding her like she was a fragile thing. Like she was precious. He had her head pressed against his chest, and she could hear his heart beating.

A reminder that he was a human man. Whatever she had said to him. However he sometimes behaved.

And she felt awash in guilt all over again. She had apologized to him once. But she wasn't sure if she had meant it. Or if it had been about soothing her own guilt, rather than truly acknowledging that she had potentially caused him pain.

She knew him well enough to know that he was…so in control of everything around him that of course his biggest vulnerability was that which he wasn't proficient at. She had stabbed him right there. Between the ribs. Right where she knew she could get to him.

And as he held her close, she felt…him.

His warmth. His strength.

She didn't care that people were staring at them.

It didn't really feel like there were any other people there at all.

She was dizzy, lightheaded. Maybe her illness was the cause of all of these feelings. Fizzing up inside of her.

Maybe it was them.

He held her, even in the elevator. They said nothing, and she was painfully aware of the sound of their breathing.

Of them.

Then they reached the top floor, and he whisked her out of the elevator, and into the penthouse.

He laid her down on the couch, and went into the kitchen, where he turned the tap which had instant hot water in it, and began to make her tea.

"Something herbal," he said. "It will settle your stomach. You like cinnamon, don't you?"

She did. Quite a bit. She usually got a sprinkle of cinnamon on top of her coffee. She often got a spice cake, or a pumpkin spice cake, or similar treat. She enjoyed a chai latte occasionally. What shocked her was that he knew that.

"I do," she said. "How do you know that?"

"I have watched you eat these many years now, have I not?"

"Yes," she said. "But I didn't think…"

"You did not think I would notice."

She winced. "No. I didn't. But that says more about me and what I think about myself than it does about what I think about you."

He arched a brow. "Does it?"

She let out a long, pained breath. "Yes. It does." She sat for a moment and stared down at the floor. "I'm sorry."

CHAPTER NINE

LUCA LOOKED AT her as if she was delusional. "You apologized already."

She swallowed. "No. I'm not sorry because I feel bad. I'm sorry now because I know that I hurt you. Worse, I tried to hurt you while telling you that you were unfeeling. I knew that you weren't, or why would I have even bothered to insult you?"

He looked stunned by that. He paused his movements, his hand still around the mug of tea. "I suppose that's true."

"I am really sorry. You didn't deserve that. I was angry and upset, and I knew that I was in a fight with you I couldn't win. I lashed out. I'm not making excuses."

He frowned. "I wanted you and the baby here with me. I don't know how to be sorry for accomplishing that."

That felt different than what he had said earlier too, even if she couldn't articulate it. But in all things, it was honest.

It wasn't that destructive, hideous catastrophe that she had lived through with her parents.

When they did nice things for her it was usually to get at the other one. Often making her feel special simply so she could be used as a pawn later. And then, when they didn't need her she didn't signify. When they were angry, she was in the way.

And they loved to deflect anger onto her.

No emotion was ever what it was presented as. But that wasn't true with him.

What he had done had been heavy-handed. But he had been clear on his goals.

He had achieved them. That was who he was.

She swallowed hard. "At least you're honest."

He frowned. "I am sorry, though, if I hurt you."

His eyes met hers, and there was honesty there. As bracing and clear as it ever was.

"Thank you." She didn't know how to articulate the ways in which he had hurt her.

She was a silly girl, that was the problem. She knew that he...that he was never going to be a man to fall madly, passionately in love with a woman.

I feel things...

No. Not because she didn't believe he had feelings, but because she believed he had one true love. And it was medicine. It was healing the world. He was a single-minded man, and she was having difficulty figuring out how he was going to slip that focus. But when he had approached her on the steps in Milan, she had been convinced that he was there for her. When really he had been there to offer her a job. She had been terrified of course, because she had been certain that he must know about the pregnancy. But…

She just didn't want to get into that, because she didn't know how to explain it. Not to him, and not to herself.

He brought her a hot mug, and placed it in her hands. Her fingertips brushed his. He had been her boss for five years.

And now he was her husband.

More than that, he was the father of the baby that was inside of her. She had been the one who was cold and clinical. She had been the one who had decided to cut him out of her life, like this was a photograph, and she could simply take scissors to it and excise him from the frame. In one brutal snip.

Just the same as she had chosen to run from him that morning after they had first made love. She was treating him like he might turn into her parents. Like he might become a monster she didn't recognize all of a sudden. He was difficult. But she understood the ways in which he was difficult. Luca had always been himself. Every inch himself. He had always been honest and up-front.

She was the one hiding.

She always had been.

Not just from him, but from everyone. Perhaps even herself.

He moved to a chair opposite her. And kept close watch on her as she took a slow sip of her tea. "This is the first time you've ever brought anything to me," she said, looking down at her cup.

"You don't work for me."

"Technically I do."

"I'm not your boss, just as you requested. It is a space to the left of me, rather than beneath me."

She snorted.

"What?"

"I *was* beneath you. That is how we ended up in this situation."

She did not know why she had brought that up. Just the mention of it made her stomach get tight. She knew his body. She could never not know it. She knew how it felt to touch him, taste him.

She might not be able to read his mind but she knew how he felt moving inside her.

That gripped her now. Held her in thrall.

"Yes," he said.

He looked thoughtful for a moment. "It is interesting. I do not often see the women that I sleep with again."

She winced. "That's sort of a bracing truth."

"Does it bother you because I was your only lover?"

She should've known that he would bring that up, and that he would be very blunt when he did. "I don't know about that, but maybe it makes it feel like we are on an equal footing."

"I would love to offer you the chance to make things equal. Because I know it isn't considered appropriate for two people who had a sexual relationship to have a power differential."

"It isn't considered appropriate," she said, trying to keep the reluctant amusement out of her voice. "But when it comes to sex people often behave inappropriately."

"I haven't. Before you. Technically, though, that night you were not my assistant."

"Oh, come now, you kissed me before midnight."

"Well, what time was it in Rome?"

She couldn't tell if he was being serious or funny. "It doesn't matter."

"It does to me. I wanted you before that night. You don't think that I was suddenly aroused for the very first time when I saw you in that dress?"

His earnestness caught her off guard, and she didn't know why it did. Because that was normal for him.

And she had to stop being shocked by it. She had to stop judging him through the lens of her parents.

He made her want to be honest in ways she never was. "Well… Tell me then. When did it start?"

"May twenty-fourth. Four years ago. It was three thirty in the afternoon. You were standing in my office. By the window. And at that time of day the light just clears the building across the way, and allows for a shaft of it to pool on the floor right by my desk. It caught your hair as you bent down, placing a cup of coffee on the desk. I saw you, and I could not look away. I realized that what I really wanted was to touch you. To rise up from my seat and kiss you. I also knew that I couldn't."

"You couldn't?"

Her breath was held fast in the center of her chest, everything in her suspended. "I thought you were a billionaire and you could do whatever you wanted."

"No, that is clearly forbidden by human resources."

"And you care about that?"

"Yes. It's there because people can get hurt if the rule is not there, and I never try to cause harm. I do it enough on accident as it is."

Her stomach twisted. "I see."

"Rules are very important."

"You know, there are a great many men who disregard those rules. Men who...don't struggle with the things that you do. They don't care."

"I do. I wouldn't have devoted my life to healing people if I didn't care about those around me. I would never have wanted to hurt you. I'm sorry that I did. But I am not sorry that you're here. I'm not even sorry that you're having my baby."

"Did you want children?"

"No. I didn't. But now that this child is growing between us, I find myself thinking about it in an entirely different way."

"How did you think of it before?"

"I didn't. I used condoms with all of my lovers, and I did not plan to ever have a relationship to progress past that point. It is a cliché, but my work has long been my mistress and I never believed it left room for there to be a significant relationship in my life."

In some ways, it was very similar to her. She hadn't thought outright that she would never have children, but of course, she didn't have a lover. So the odds of accidentally landing herself with the child were zero. "But now you want one?"

"I want this child. Perhaps that doesn't make sense. I know that the baby is the size of a raspberry."

"Of course you do."

"Anything medical, I am expert on. I also know that there is a chance that the child won't make it to term."

"I'd rather not think about that."

"Really? I would've thought that in some ways it would be easier for you to miscarry."

He wasn't trying to be cruel, but still, it hit her like a brutal blow. "Well, maybe you're right. But I don't feel that way. I haven't felt that way. Not even for a moment in the beginning. In fact…" She had cried. She had wept like she was dying, and then she had felt afraid. Afraid that her initial sorrow would mean that she was robbed of the life growing inside of her. It had been the single most contradictory, frightening thing she had ever been through. But in the end, she had been clear on the fact that she wanted the baby. That wasn't ambiguous. Not in the least.

"I don't want you to lose the baby either."

"I have terrible parents," she said.

She had never spoken of her parents. Not to anyone. "I mean, really terrible. They were so toxic, with each other and with me. What they did was tantamount to emotional abuse. It's why I'm so good at putting a mask on every day of my life. It's why I don't like being vulnerable. Or caught unawares. It's why I always pretend like I know exactly what's going on, even when I don't, because what I know is that when certain people think they can get to you, then they will. And if you show them what you really feel, they'll manipulate it. I learned that from them. I didn't think that I was like them. Until

I lashed out at you yesterday. So now I know that when things get difficult, I'm not necessarily at my best."

"I didn't know that," he said. "About your parents."

"Of course you didn't. I didn't tell anyone. I tried to leave that life, that version of myself in Indiana."

"I knew you were from Indiana because it's in your file. But you have never spoken of it."

"Because there's nothing to say. I didn't want to be that girl anymore so I moved to a new country and became a different one."

"An extraordinary feat," he said. "Truly. I only know how to be the man that I am and that comes with its own set of issues."

"I know."

They were silent for a moment. "I would like to let you go and even things out between us. In regard to lovers. But I can't. I cannot be fair or impartial when it comes to the subject of you allowing other men to touch you. I cannot be…the way I usually am. So perhaps in that regard I have become new. Or maybe something has become new inside of me. Probably in the time since May twenty-fourth four years ago."

There was something so earnest and lovely in those words. Maybe not everyone would see it, but she did.

She took a sip of the cinnamon-flavored tea and leaned back on the couch. She began to feel sleepy and set the cup on the table beside her.

He picked it up, and put a coaster beneath it, but didn't scold her. "Rest," he said. "I will be here when you wake."

When she did wake an hour or so later, it occurred to her that it was a singular thing for him to promise. He should be at work today. He didn't go.

The next morning when she woke unwell, he didn't go to work either. Or the next day, or the next. It was a complete and total rearranging of his routine and no one had ever, not once, disrupted their life on her behalf. She didn't know what to make of it. Only that it made her sore right at the center of her chest.

She crept into the kitchen to find Luca cooking. As if he didn't have a full staff for such a thing. As if he couldn't magic something up with the snap of his fingers.

"What are you making?" she asked, hearing how small her voice sounded even in her own ears.

"An omelet. Protein. Vegetables."

She thought she probably shouldn't tell him she had no interest in protein or vegetables, and instead wanted cookies all the time. Given that Luca was so very Luca he would probably frown on that.

Processed sugar for his baby? Never.

Except the baby was also hers. So there would be sugar.

The idea of trying to live with this man, compromise with him, raise a child with him, was suddenly daunting.

She sat down at the kitchen island and leaned forward. "I will eat the omelet. And thank you for it. But right now I usually crave sweets in the morning."

"Unhealthy," he said.

He was so predictable.

"Be that as it may," she said. "It's what I want. And while I'm all for health, happiness is part of health."

"Not in a practical sense."

"Actually, yes, Luca. In a practical sense. We aren't just bodies rattling around the physical world. We're more than that." She cleared her throat. "I'd have thought that you'd know that more than anyone. Considering how the order of the world affects your mind. That's not physical. Not having three notebooks on a plane isn't necessary for physical health, but you don't *feel* right if you don't have them."

"And you are trying to make the case that you don't feel right if you don't have cakes?"

"Indeed."

"Hmm."

"I'll have the omelet," she conceded.

"You are welcome."

"I did thank you," she pointed out. "But I had the thought we're probably going to have to discuss the ways we're different from each other, and the ways that might express itself in our lives and in our...parenting styles." She cleared her throat, wanting to be careful now. "I am actually not trying to say anything unkind, but you're a very particular man."

"That isn't unkind. It's true."

"Yes, but I used the truth to be hurtful the other day and I'm sorry for it. So I'm trying to prove I'm not out here using elements of what's honest as a sword. I'm just trying to look ahead."

"All right, tell me what you're thinking."

He put the omelet in front of her and her stomach growled. "I don't always eat healthy. I like sweets."

"I like sweets," he said.

She narrowed her eyes. "I have never seen you eat sweets."

"Everything in moderation."

"Well, I'm going to eat them. And I don't want to overwhelm a child with data on what every medical journal the world over says about diet."

"Fair," he said. "But I will require that it is taken into account. I'm not opposed to treats but we must consult the *World Pediatrics Journal* regarding diet as a baseline."

"Most parents won't be doing that."

"I am not most parents."

She couldn't argue that point. She didn't even want to because then he set a mug of herbal tea next to her and it made her feel like she was glowing inside. It made her feel cared for.

No one had ever cared for her before. She had done a lot of caring for other people. And maybe it was a really small thing. Breakfast and a cup of tea. A couple of days of missed work. And yet, for him it wasn't. She knew that.

"If it's that important to you," she said. "It's very important to me that whatever is going on between the two of us, we never let it spill over onto our baby. Our child. Luca, there are going to be times when you frustrate me. But I never want our child to be aware of that.

I never want for your mood or my mood to become their problem."

He nodded slowly. "Agreed."

"And it's important that our child comes first. That is going to mean that sometimes you have to make sacrifices with work. But I don't want a father for my baby that's going to be half there and half gone."

"You were more than willing to have me be all gone."

"Sometimes I think that's easier."

He looked away. "No," he said. "It isn't. Because when my mother was all gone, then there was nothing soft left. There was no one left who looked at me and everything I was and smiled. I lost every ounce of support I had once had. I would have rather had her one day a month. One day a year. I'm glad I had her for the time that I did. Had I not had her at all, what would I be?"

She hated thinking of him like that. Alone. Vulnerable. She did feel protective of him, in spite of everything. She felt...

You care about him.

She tried to swallow past the lump in her throat.

"Right," she said, her throat scratchy. "But your mother didn't choose to leave you. You remember your mother so fondly because of all the good things that she did for you. Because of the good she saw in you. And I assume because you were the most important thing in her life. You and I do important things. Having a baby doesn't erase that, or negate it. Neither of us should give up what we love. But if we were to make a list of the things that we loved..."

"The child should be the first thing."

"Yes. And at the very least they should feel that they are."

"Are you suggesting again that I'm going to have difficulty loving a child?"

She snorted. "I'm leaving space for both of us to have to spend time adjusting to this. We both love work."

"You love work?" he asked.

"I spent five years giving you and this company the entirety of myself. Why would you think I didn't love work?"

"You did quit."

"Because I didn't love being nothing more than an assistant."

"You say that as if you were inconsequential, and indeed I believe that you think you were to me. You weren't. You are…insulted that I came after you to offer you your job back, as if it was a small thing." He shook his head. "I chased you down. I put my pride away. I cared absolutely nothing for it, because I needed to have you back. It was essential. Important. I cannot think that you do not know that."

She hadn't. Well, she hadn't thought of it that way. But of course, there was actually no real separation between Luca the man and his job. What she had taken as a weak showing in the face of their passion had likely been altogether powerful for him. He had gone to her because he was admitting that he couldn't handle life without her.

"Well. I do care. And I'm sorry that I didn't see the

gesture for what it was. I can now. So let me try and explain to you… I left because I could have actually stayed your assistant forever. But it wasn't what I set out to do. It wasn't the schooling that I got, it wasn't… That job was my everything, and so were you. I needed it to change. But now things have changed again. We have to be willing to change with them."

"Even if it means eating omelets?"

She turned her fork sideways and cut a bite off with a fearsome motion. "This isn't a permanent change. I'm simply indulging you for the day."

"I consider myself extremely fortunate."

He was teasing her again. So unlike him, and yet, more frequent now than it had been before.

"And thank you," she said. "For taking care of me."

"Of course."

CHAPTER TEN

LUCA DID RETURN to work the next day. There were things to see to, and they were of utmost importance. But then, everything in this job was. Still, he'd had to put everything aside out of concern for Polly's health and well-being for the past few days. At first it had given him no small measure of discomfort. To discard his routine. To be away from his work for an extended period of time—not that he hadn't checked in, or completed tasks in his home office—but eventually, he had realized that it was a good thing.

He wanted things to be as Polly had said.

He wanted to rearrange his life.

He felt a powerful connection to this child. This child who wasn't yet born. He could already feel the desperate pull to rearrange everything so that he could be a good father.

Not the sort of father who would reject and shame his child. A father who would care for them no matter what.

He found himself thinking about Polly, back at the penthouse. He found his mind more there than in the office, and given that he had not been into the office for some days prior to this, it surprised him. More than that, he found he wanted to hold on to this.

It was a rare thing, this sort of moment when he could hold multiple thoughts in his mind. Multiple concerns.

Yes, single-minded focus got a fair amount of things accomplished. But he wanted to be single-minded in his parenting as well. He wanted to hold his child with him, even as he went about his day.

In many ways, he did that with his mother.

She was his motivation. His reason.

But practically, she required nothing of him.

She was a memory, and nothing more. Living for a memory of a person was much simpler than figuring out how to foster a relationship with a person who was here.

She had a doctor appointment scheduled for later that same day, and he made a call down to the office. He let them know that he would be attending, and that he wished to help conduct the tests and exams. No one argued, even though it was unorthodox, because he was Dr. Luca Salvatore, and his reputation in medicine preceded him.

He was eager for Polly to return to the office, because he did not like her absence. Even though she would be taking another job, she would be here, and things would feel better. They would feel right. He did decide to call her and let her know that he would be at her appointment.

"I should've thought to include you," she said.

She had been extraordinarily different with him these past days. When she had apologized to him, because she had hurt his feelings, and not to make herself feel better, it had shifted something inside of him.

No other person had ever treated him that way. Not since his mother.

His mother had known and understood that he had so many feelings, and that they were complicated. That he didn't know how people expected him to express them, nor did he care.

But she had seen him. And he didn't think that Polly had this entire time, but she certainly did now.

He hadn't thought he cared about that.

It hadn't occurred to him that it might be a nice thing to have someone understand him.

He had decided that he by and large didn't need emotional connections with people, but he was going to be a father, and that meant he was going to have to forge an emotional connection with his child. So perhaps it was only a good thing to practice by forging emotional connections with other people.

And trying to get a sense for what it felt like when they had them with him.

"I was happy to include myself," he said.

"Yes. Well. I suppose that's not surprising."

"I will see you in an hour."

"See you then."

They rode in the same car over to the private doctor's office. They were taken into a room where the doctor did an initial Doppler check to establish that the fetal heart rate was normal. All was well, and he felt the tension in his chest ease that he hadn't been aware was there.

"And an ultrasound," he said.

"We typically don't—"

He looked at the doctor. "I am aware. But I would like to have one done. I called ahead."

"Of course, Dr. Salvatore."

They were ushered into the sonogram room, and he introduced himself to the technician. "I would like to perform the sonogram," he said.

Polly looked at him, her eyes wide. "What?"

"I'm a doctor."

"You aren't an ultrasound technician," Polly said.

"No. But I have the necessary qualifications and knowledge."

"I don't want you to do it," she said.

"I told you that I—"

"Yes," she said. "You are a doctor. But you're not *my* doctor. You're the father of my baby, and that's it."

"Is that all?"

He felt…scalded by that.

"Yes, Luca," she said. "That is all."

"You're acting like I don't have feelings again," he said.

She shook her head. "I'm really not. I'm asking you to be reasonable. To consider if it's a typical thing for a father to be in charge of running the ultrasound, or if you should trust the people who make this their exper-tise to do their jobs."

He scowled. Mostly because he could see that she was potentially right. He still wanted to be the one to do this. He wanted to be the one to make sure that everything was okay. It was important to him.

"You can stand there," she said. "And look. And if you see something of concern, why don't you ask the woman to linger there."

The ultrasound tech was looking between them and Luca didn't bother to try and read her expression. He didn't care. He only knew that he was irritated, in part because she might even be right. And even if she wasn't, he could see that it was going to benefit him to bend here. He didn't want to bend. Medicine was the way he cared. It was all he was.

And yet again, Polly didn't understand that. She didn't understand that for him this was caring.

How else was he supposed to show it?

He wanted to be in control of everything happening. He understood that. He didn't see what was wrong with it, though. That was the problem. She was being stubborn right now.

The ultrasound tech readied the equipment, and Polly looked at him. "What?"

"I'm going to have to put the gown on."

"Yes," the tech said. "It's going to be an internal ultrasound."

"In that case, Polly must be certain that she wants one. I directed this, but didn't think the implications through."

"It's okay," she said. "I would like to see the baby."

"You're certain?"

He had been controlling this, from the beginning.

And he logically knew the way that ultrasounds work, but he hadn't fully considered what that might mean to Polly, or that she might find it invasive. He did sometimes shut off the full implications of things. He knew that to be true.

And he felt regretful that he had perhaps inadvertently caused the situation when what he had been trying to do was make himself feel better.

"I do want to see," she said. "But I need you to turn around right now."

He did, though he didn't understand why she was being shy now when he had seen her naked.

He was struck then by a completely unexpected arrow of lust. He had done a very good job not thinking of her that way. She had been poorly. And he had been obsessed with the idea of having her back at his side. Of sorting out all of these things pertaining to the baby. Pertaining to them.

He hadn't thought of that night. Deliberately. Because he had been intent on hiring her back. But suddenly, it was replaying itself in his mind. Vivid. Intense.

He curled his fingers into fists, and waited. Listening for the sounds of her disrobing.

This feeling, of course, was exactly why they were in this situation.

This feeling and May twenty-fourth.

And that night.

He really hadn't used a condom.

He still couldn't… He couldn't quite believe it. He couldn't remember it. Couldn't even remember thinking about it. And that was completely outside of his experience. Contraception, protecting both himself and his lover had always been paramount rules.

But he hadn't thought of rules when he was with her. Not even a little bit.

"You can turn around now," she said.

He did. She was lying on the table with a sheet draped over her knees, and the angle he was at prevented him from seeing anything.

"Sorry," the tech said. "This part is always cold. And a little bit uncomfortable."

He couldn't see what was going on beneath the sheet, but he knew. Because he knew the procedure well.

He found that he could not entirely find the doctor in the scenario though, and that was odd.

He felt a knot of worry, concern about her potential discomfort.

These were things he had never felt when he had done residency. And while he didn't practice medicine in the traditional sense, he had learned to do it.

He had always felt disconnected from the experience the patient was having, but not now.

The black-and-white screen flickered, and then, he could not tear his eyes away. It took a moment, but then he was able to see a fluttering. The amniotic sac. The embryo itself. "There he is," he said, unable to hold back a smile. Unable to be rational. Because this was such an early stage of development. Anything could happen. And yet he didn't feel detached. He didn't feel as if he knew he should. He felt something broad, expansive growing inside of him.

Love.

Deep and intense, along with it the desire to protect. Fiercely.

This was beyond the scope of anything he had ever known before. It was beyond him.

"Incredible," he said.

Even though it wasn't. It was run-of-the-mill. It was average. People did this every day.

But he could not find a single thing that felt commonplace about it.

Because Polly was carrying his baby in her womb. This was the result of their night of passion, his loss of control. The culmination of a hundred things that felt unlikely and yet right at the same time.

He felt…gratitude that transcended logic. He felt something that he could not easily name. He felt everything. All at once. Like the cover had been lifted on something bright and intense inside of him, and now that it was revealed it couldn't be hidden.

He looked at Polly, because suddenly it was very important that he see her face. That he see what she was feeling.

Her eyes glittered, but he couldn't figure out what exactly the tears were for. Tears, he found, were a constellation. They could contain many truths. They were never half so simple as sadness, or happiness. They spoke of intensity. Overwhelmed. Sometimes he thought it wasn't that he couldn't understand what other people were feeling, but that people were very quick to simplify feelings. Tried to put one name to them when they had a depth, and all-encompassing nature that was different than simply happy or sad.

Often he was angry because he was afraid. Often he was happy, but tired, because that happiness had come at a cost. From many sleepless nights. Right now he was grateful, but with it came a measure of awe. Of uncertainty.

He moved closer to the screen then, and began to examine the black-and-white image. Because emotions might be something that he found difficult and complex, but there was nothing complex about the physical.

To his eye, everything on the scan looked normal. "Go back," he said.

The ultrasound tech looked at him. "To where?"

"I would like to get a look at the heart chambers."

"It is very early."

"I would still like it. Along with a full panel of blood work."

"I don't order blood work. The doctor will, if she sees a need."

"I see the need."

"Luca," said Polly. "Let's discuss this later."

She was speaking to him like he was a naughty child. And that irritated him as much as he had been awestruck the moment before.

The ultrasound tech moved back to the heart, and he watched. Watched it move. Flutter.

"Thank you."

When they were finished, Polly demanded he turn around again so that she could get dressed. At that point, the tech left the room.

"You didn't have to be that difficult," she said.

"I'm not being difficult."

"I didn't know that you were coming here and you were going to try and act as a doctor. I thought that you were here as the father."

"I was," he said. "But for me the two things are not different. Because nothing inside of me is different."

"You cannot be this obtuse. Surely you understand why it's frustrating for a professional to have somebody looming over them like that."

"It was not looming."

"You were," she said.

They exited the exam room, and went out into the front of the office. She made a new appointment.

"That is during my workday."

"I don't care."

They walked out, and a car was waiting for them. She got into the back, not waiting for him to let her in.

He slid in beside her. "Did you need to be told that I was going to want to have involvement in the medical side of this?"

"No. I didn't need to be told. We needed to talk about it. Because what you are wanting to do, is it normal?"

"I'm not normal," he said, feeling at the end of this. At the end of himself. "You know that. You have worked with me for five years. What about me has ever said normal human being."

"I don't think of you that way," she said. "I don't think of you as being weird. Or abnormal. But this isn't normal. And when something is going to be abnormal, then surely it must occur to you on some level that you have to actually speak to the other person involved in the situation before you go…being that."

"If I knew, if I had that level of clarity, then maybe I would. But it seems perfectly logical to me, and I don't understand how it doesn't to you. I am a medical doctor. I did a residency. I have done all the schooling, and all the training. I also have a doctorate in medical research, and have been responsible for many advancements in the field of medicine over the past decade. You know this. Why would you think that I would…not want my eyes, my expertise, my opinion involved in the single most important medical event that has ever occurred in my life."

She said nothing for a moment. "You're afraid, aren't you?"

"I'm not afraid."

"Yes, you are. You thought that I was sick when you came to Milan. You're afraid of things going wrong for people that you… I don't know, do you care about me, Luca?"

"How can you say that? My life would not function without you in it, and you are well aware of this."

"All right. It's all about how functional your life is or isn't because I am in it. I forgot. That's not caring." She was silent for a moment. "You care about the baby, don't you?"

"I do care," he said. "I want you to allow me to care in the way that I know how to show it."

She looked at him, something in her expression softening. "That's admirable. But you also have to care in a way that the other person can receive it. It feels stressful for me. To have you be… There in an official capacity. There is a doctor. I want you there as…"

"Your husband? Because you don't want me to be your husband in any other capacity. It is you who are inconsistent."

Just then, the car pulled up to his building. He got out, and this time, he was the one who didn't pay her any mind. He was the one who didn't pause.

He walked into the building, a tangle of anger growling around his chest. Yet again, a whole layer of emotions he couldn't quite so neatly define. But anger was certainly the hottest part. It made him burn.

She caught up to him by the time the elevator doors opened, and she got inside with him.

"Are you suggesting that you want to be my husband?" she asked when the doors closed.

"I asked you to marry me. You were the one who issued edicts about our physical relationship. And about what we would and would not be."

"Can't you see why?"

"Yes," he said. "Because it is impossible to approach any of this fully logically. And I would prefer it if we could."

"We're human. Not Vulcan."

"I've been accused of being a Vulcan more than once."

"I know. By me. But you told me that isn't how you are. You have to find a way to let that part of you come forward. The part that feels."

"It's uncomfortable."

"Incubating your baby is pretty uncomfortable. I don't know if you've noticed. But I've been rather unwell."

The elevator reached its destination and she swept out.

And it was like everything in him went blank. It was like everything was calm. Clear. He saw her.

Just as he had May twenty-fourth at three thirty in the afternoon. When she walked into his apartment the sunlight tangled with her hair. Illuminating it. Casting it in gold.

Feeling.

Yes. He could open himself up to feeling. To all of it. To be a better husband, to be a better father.

But she had said that she didn't want what he felt.

Now she *wanted* his feelings.

She was entirely and utterly inconsistent. But more than that, she was radiant. More than that, he wanted her.

So she wanted feeling. She was going to get his feeling.

He crossed the space, and wrapped his arm around her waist. And before she could say anything, before she could beg him or protest, he lowered his head and claimed her mouth with his.

CHAPTER ELEVEN

HE REMEMBERED THIS. From that night. This passion. A conflagration, that was far beyond anything he had ever experienced before. Kissing had never been this. Desire had never been this. Need had never been an all-consuming driving urge that swamped his thoughts and made them go blank.

It was like sanctuary.

All day, every day, he was bombarded. The world around him was too loud. The feelings inside of him were too big. The thoughts inside his head so fast it was difficult to grab hold of one of them. And they never stopped. Never.

Except now. It was like everything whittled itself down into one singular point.

All that mattered was the sound of their breathing. The feel of her mouth beneath his. The way that her body felt beneath his hands, warm and supple, and all that he truly desired.

There were no thoughts. Because they were unnecessary.

And the feeling was only good.

And yet, nothing half so simple as good.

Sharp and poignant. Decadent and punishing. A revelation and a condemnation.

A baptism and hellfire.

He paused for a moment, for a breath. He pulled away and he looked at her. He waited. For her to say no. For her to pull away.

She didn't. Instead she stretched up on her toes, wrapped her hand around the back of his head and pulled him down for a kiss.

Another one. This one more intense than the last.

Her hands were demanding, her mouth even more so. He tasted her deeply, his tongue sliding against hers, his arousal hot.

Overwhelming.

But in a good way, rather than in the way the world could feel all too often.

In this moment, there was no fear. No medicine. No discoveries yet uncharted that went anywhere beyond them.

And she… She was a discovery yet to be made. Yes, he had been with her once before. He had seen her naked. Answered the questions that he'd had about his assistant. But he was a curious man. And he could never be satisfied with just one panel of evidence. With just one moment of discovery. He needed to go deeper. He needed to find it all.

He needed to examine every angle. Every line. Every possibility.

And so slowly, he began to take her clothes off of

her body. He gave thanks for the fact that it was three thirty in the afternoon. But the sun was shining down through the window.

That he would finally see her skin and all this golden light.

Because it was what he had wanted all these years. It was what he had denied himself because of propriety and rules.

But he would not deny himself now. Not anymore.

He realized then that he was entirely comprised of self-denial. Because he was so careful to never make a misstep. So careful to steer clear of doing the inappropriate. Of being wrong. Of showing that he cared more, of showing that he hurt more.

Of drawing attention to the real ways that he was abnormal.

But not here. Not now. He would allow himself this. To want more. To need more.

To need her.

So he unwrapped her like she was a sacred, precious gift, and he let himself get drunk on the glory of her every curve. The glorious softness of her skin. Her breasts were larger, rounder than they had been that first night they were together.

Her nipples were tight, a delicious berry pink that called to his appetites. And he decided to indulge them. He lowered his head and slid his tongue over that tightened bud, growling as he did. She gasped, holding his head to her, and arching against him. He sucked her deep, trying to assuage the roaring need drowning out the sound of everything but his heartbeat. Feeling. He was all feeling now.

This was what she wanted. Him. Like this.

She could have it.

And so would he.

In all of its splendor. In all of its glory.

Because he could feel the air, skimming over his skin, a heightened sense of need and desire and being alive that he wasn't sure anyone else felt. But he did.

And right now, it was a good thing. Because her touch coupled with that sensitivity was all the drug he would ever need.

And someday, if he was ever found lying on the floor, addled by addiction, it would be her.

That addiction would be her.

He had been obsessed with her from the beginning.

And he had blinded himself to what that meant.

Because it was this. Always. From moment one.

She pushed at his shoulders, and he allowed her to do so, moving away from her. "It's my turn," she said, beginning to tug at the buttons on his shirt.

She undressed him, her fingers clumsy, and he found that endearing, because Polly was so rarely clumsy. She was always in charge. The master of everything, everything around him, all the details, his whole life.

But she was trembling now.

"Are you afraid?" he asked.

She shook her head. "I'm shaking because I want you."

And this was why emotions were so difficult.

Because sometimes shaking was fear. And sometimes it was this.

He gripped her chin between his thumb and forefinger and leaned in, kissing her again.

She pushed the shirt from his shoulders and let it fall to the floor. She looked at him with the same sort of greed he knew had been on his face when he had examined her.

A triumph.

Physically, he had always been attractive to women.

It was everything else about him that created difficulties.

It was one reason he was very obsessive in his workout routines. Health being a primary goal and focus, of course. But, anything that made things easier was of course a boon. And he had found his physique absolutely made things easier.

She clearly appreciated his work.

She put her hand on his chest, let her fingertips drift down his abdomen. He closed his eyes, growled.

This was what it was like to feel. To only feel. To not think. To not worry about what he did next. To not worry how he would be received.

Some people felt this way all the time.

He was all right if he only felt that here. With her. It was a gift.

And one he would never take lightly.

He stripped the rest of her clothes away, and she did the same for him. And both of them were brilliantly, gloriously naked in that afternoon sun. He kissed her.

Her neck, her collarbone, down the valley of her breasts. Her stomach. He lifted her up from the ground and set her gently on the edge of the couch, where he draped her legs over his shoulders and began to lick into her. Deeply, ravenously.

Her taste haunted his dreams.

He had wanted no one since her.

And while it was not entirely unheard of for him to close off his libido when it was convenient, it had never gone and done so on its own without his permission.

And yet with her…

She was what he wanted. Not sex. No other woman would do. He wanted her.

He licked her until she cried out his name. Until he felt her give up her control. Until he felt her release wash over them both.

And then he moved over her on the couch, lifting her thigh over his hip and claiming her in one smooth stroke.

Her fingernails dug into his shoulders.

Pain. Pleasure.

All the layers of humanity.

He began to move, his need utterly blotting out everything else. Her breath in his ear, the press of her breasts against his chest. The tight, wet heat of her body as she enveloped him.

"Polly," he said. He said her name over and over again like an incantation, a prayer.

And then he felt his release begin to rise inside of him. He held it back as long as he could.

He didn't want this to end.

He wanted her.

This moment.

Forever.

But then she cried out his name, arching against him, her internal muscles pulsing around him, and he was lost.

He gritted his teeth, buried his face in her neck, and came hard.

"Don't run from me," he said, eyes blazing into hers after the storm subsided.

"I won't," she said softly.

He moved away from her slowly, and then went into the bathroom to get a damp cloth.

He brought it back, and kept his eyes on hers as he pressed it between her legs.

"Thank you," she said. "But it was…fine without."

"I just want to take care of you," he said. "And I can acknowledge that the way I tried to do that earlier didn't look like care to you."

She closed her eyes. "It did. But it made me uncomfortable. I could see where you were coming from. But…"

"I'm not allowed to always have my way."

"No," she said. "That's part of sharing your life with somebody."

"That's probably why I have never done it before."

"I haven't really either, Luca."

"You said that you were a virgin," he said.

"Yes," she said. "I was." She moved the cloth away, and sat up, wrapping her hand around his bicep. "Because I had made a life for myself where I had all the control, and I liked it. I didn't see the point of inviting another person in."

She sighed heavily. "But that's only part of the story. I also had a job and a boss that were completely all-consuming. And I couldn't imagine being with another man while I was so enmeshed in your life."

"Because I took up all your personal time?"

"That was part of it. Because of course nobody wants to be in the middle of an intimate moment and have their boss call and demand they tell him which tie he ought to wear for his next speech. But it was only part of it. I wanted you, Luca. And I couldn't want somebody else while I wanted you."

"Oh," he said.

"Did you really not know?"

"I really didn't. But then, you were my assistant, and that made you off-limits. And even though I had moments of failure in that area, I did my best to close off my thoughts of you. Now I'm glad that I don't have to."

She sighed heavily. "What are we going to do? Because if we introduce sex, then we are really in a marriage. And the potential to hurt each other…"

"We are really in a marriage. We got legally married."

"I get that. I mean, I get that you see it that way. But I wanted to protect myself. Keep something that was mine. What am I going to do if things sour between us? You have all the power, and you already threatened to take our child away."

"I will never threaten something like that again. I'm sorry."

"Are you sorry because it scares me?"

"Yes. I am. I'm sorry that I used my position to terrorize you. That was the whole point of not having sex with you when you were my assistant. And then I did it anyway. It was the only way that I knew how to try and convince you to come with me."

"Last time I asked you said you weren't sorry."

"As I got my way. But now I can see how I ought to be sorry about how I did it. About not giving you time. Not trusting you to come to the best conclusion."

"Neither of us knows how to be in a relationship."

He shook his head. "No. But we have a great many things to learn. And you are having my child. Also, I want you. I never wanted anyone the way that I want you. I've never forgotten myself. I've never forgotten to think. But when you touch me it's like everything fades away. It's like I understand…what it's like to be somebody else for a while. I suddenly don't feel consumed in an obsessive sort of way. Everything feels simple. And good. Like the only thing in my life is your hands on me. When normally I feel pulled in a hundred different directions all the time. I want that. I want more of it."

"But you're not in love with me," she said.

"No."

One of the many emotions he had no experience with, and no burning desire to try and explore. It would be far too much.

But he wanted her. And logically it made sense. It

made a perfect kind of sense. They were already having a child. This connection between them existed. Why take all the energy it would require to suppress it? That would be madness. And he was not a man given to madness.

On purpose. Because he'd always had the feeling it could take him if it tried.

If he let it.

"I can't promise you the same thing that another man might. But then, from what you told me about your parents you know that what starts as love can end as something entirely horrific."

"I do."

"So I am not offering you that. But I am telling you that I will try to learn to care in a way that you can receive. And that I will always be honest with you."

"I know that," she said. "Because for all that you frustrate me sometimes, you have always been honest with me. Always. You never tried to manipulate me. You strong-armed me so that you could have your way, but it was entirely obvious what you were doing. You never promised me one thing and delivered another."

"I won't do it now. But I cannot see a future where we continue to live together, work together, raise a child together, and we ignore this thing between us."

She sighed heavily. "But sexual attraction doesn't last forever."

"No. But decisions can. Especially decisions that you make every day. I want our child to have the best life possible. And even when my father was himself, having my mother in the house made it better. You need that other parent. For when the one is unable to do their best. You need both. Just in case one needs to be lifted up. And I fear very much that I might need that."

"Just decide that you're going to be as single-minded when it comes to being a good father as you are with anything else. If you do that, I'm confident that you're going to succeed."

"Yes," he said, looking out the window. "I can do that."

"You don't have to be afraid."

"But I still want you there. I have always wanted you there. Since you were my assistant. You made every-thing better. You always have. And you will make this better too."

"Okay. Okay, Luca. Let's give this a try. Real mar-riage. Raising our child."

"Thank you." He leaned in and he kissed her. And when their lips touched, there was nothing but feeling. "That's all I want."

"Me too."

CHAPTER TWELVE

LUCA HAD GONE back to work after their afternoon love-making session. She wasn't even really mad about it. Really, she wasn't mad about it at all. Because if he didn't do something that felt quintessentially Luca she might start to get concerned about him. But she didn't want to sit at home, and she hadn't started her job at Salvatore yet. Really, she wasn't entirely clear on what she was going to do. But for the first time in her memory that wasn't the most all-consuming thing on her mind.

They were committing to… Well, in his mind it was real marriage. Love and romance and the like didn't seem to signify for him. And she wondered why it should matter to her at all. Because he was right. Her parents' marriage had started real enough. She didn't know anything about the relationship between his parents but he made it sound like his father was useless. At least, when it came to Luca. So what did it matter if people got married for conventional reasons? It didn't guarantee happiness. Why should love mean anything to her?

It never had before. But maybe that was part of the

problem. She had avoided the concept of marriage and childbearing because she hadn't wanted anything that looked like her parents. But now that she was married, now that she had a child on the way, she couldn't help but wonder if...

It really would be a terrible thing to love him.

Except, she couldn't look at him anymore and see the remote man that she had once imagined existed behind that armor he wore all day every day. That man of steel who was so committed to work that everything else was an inconvenience.

No.

He was passionate. He was hot. A fire blazing inside the shape of a man.

How had she ever imagined that he was anything less?

He was... He was a study in contradictions. Because he could be so uncompromising, and then when she called him on it he often apologized. Unless he didn't. Unless he stood firm because he simply couldn't see what she was saying.

But for all that he often did that first, then he would normally try. Try to understand where she was coming from, try to see where she was coming from. And now he was saying he was committed to trying to care for her in the way that she could receive it.

Change, for him, was harder than it was for most and she knew that. She'd felt like he hadn't cared for her, and now here he was rearranging his carefully curated life for her.

She had known few people who listened quite that well. Who cared so much about doing the right thing.

She decided that she needed to get some fresh air. She got dressed, and left the scene of her indignity, going down to the Roman streets and letting herself blend into the crowd.

She had immediately loved that about Rome. The anonymity of it.

The way that she felt like she could blend, and more than that, the way that she felt like she could be anything she wanted to be.

She had been so trapped in Indiana. On that same street, in that same house.

Her life hadn't been small because she lived in a small town, her life had been small because she had been crushed in her parents' fists.

She knew a shiver of fear as she tried to imagine living life with Luca. Yes. There was a scenario wherein she could see herself being crushed.

But she didn't have to be. She could keep talking to him. Especially if he kept listening.

She walked into a couple of clothing stores and looked at the offerings. She loved all the beautiful clothes in the city. But unfortunately, considering that she was about to change and expand in several different ways, there really was no point in buying fashion.

She thought wistfully for a moment about what could've been. That life in Milan. At the fashion house, where she would undoubtedly be getting free clothing as part of her job.

All she could muster up was wistfulness. There was no sadness. There was no regret.

She hadn't been as happy doing that as she had thought she might be. And really, the day she had taken the pregnancy test, everything changed.

She hadn't realized all the ways it had changed yet, but it had.

She was different.

Her future looked different.

Maybe, if she was going to be living in Milan a single unencumbered girl without a baby on the way, that job would've been perfect.

You would've had to have never met Luca.

She sighed heavily.

Yes. She would've had to have not met Luca. Because meeting him had changed her life. Forget sleeping with him.

There was something about him. Something that had grabbed hold of her and refused to let go the first moment they had met.

He was just so singularly him.

And on paper, all the things he was should be mainly annoying.

She walked out of the boutique, and continued down the street. And then, through one of the reflective windows, she spotted a little red car.

It was a toy store. There were teddy bears and a large, magical-looking tree positioned in the window. A little village. And that red car.

It called to her. Because it spoke of Luca.

Yes. He could be infuriating. Yes, on paper, he was a disaster of a boss, and not much better as a man.

But he was also a boy once. A boy who had loved cars. Until his mother had died and all he had been able to care about was how to keep someone else from experiencing that kind of pain.

His whole life had been consumed in that pain. And he had let go of that thing that he loved most. In order to give himself over to his mission.

She found herself walking into the toy store without thinking. Because she wanted to see to him. The way that she had as his assistant, but something else, something deeper.

She asked to see the car, and turned it over in her hands. Yes. She needed to get this for him. Her chest felt tight as she paid, and had the car put in a little box, and gift wrapped.

It occurred to her then, as she walked out of the store with the car in a jaunty yellow bag, that she did know how to care for him.

She had been doing it for five years. All those things that people were so quick to call ridiculous, she recognized were integral to him.

Like when she had gotten angry at the flight attendant for not understanding why he needed his notebooks.

They mattered to her. As they mattered to him.

They weren't inconveniences. And they weren't him being particular. Not really. It was what he needed. Nobody else was him. So why did other people get to make proclamations about what he should change, what was important, and what was an incidental?

Yes, there was a place for them to compromise. Of course there was. Because she didn't need to be cared for in a way that worked for her. She had lived with parents who didn't care for her at all. But that wasn't Luca. And so asking him to meet her in the middle didn't seem outrageous. But it also meant seeing him as he was.

But she had never had any trouble with that.

He could be frustrating, certainly. And she felt then, as she walked down the lovely, sunny street, that it was fair to be frustrated even by things he couldn't easily change. Because when you lived with somebody that was the state of things.

But she didn't feel anymore like there was Luca, a typical man, and all of the little quirks that made him into something more of a project.

They were all him. They didn't separate.

And so caring about those things was caring about him.

And she wanted him to have the car.

Because she mourned for the lighter things that he had cared about once, that he couldn't afford to care about when his life became something heavy. When she got back to the penthouse, he wasn't there. She decided that she was going to cook for him since he had done so much of that for her over the past week.

He liked to cook. It was something that she had always found interesting about him. Because most single men didn't seem to enjoy that quite so much. And a man of his status could certainly afford somebody to do it for him.

But of course he didn't really like a surplus of strangers in his home. Because everything needed to be where he wanted it. And that seemed quintessentially him.

She decided to make pasta with olive oil, tomatoes and some Parmesan. Simple, but she had found since moving to Rome that simple was her preference. When the ingredients were so spectacular, there was nothing not to like about simple.

She hummed as she put the food together, as she made a salad.

And by the time he walked through the door, she had everything ready, with her gift for him at the center of the table.

His eyes met hers, and he smiled. It was brilliant.

She could count on one hand how many times she had seen him smile in an unguarded fashion, and every single one of those times prior to this it had been in connection to a medical discovery.

This was the first time that smile had ever been directed at her.

Oh, dear.

She really liked him. A lot.

But imagine loving him.

Only a foolish idiot would love him.

Really.

She swallowed hard. "I made dinner."

"I can see that."

"I got you a present. But we should eat first."

MILLIE ADAMS   163

"I want to open my present," he said, looking suddenly like a petulant child, and her heart squeezed. Because she wondered if he had ever been able to afford to be a petulant child.

"No," she said in her best stern matron voice. "You have to eat first."

He growled. But sat down. He dished his plate, and she was walking by him to go do the same, when he grabbed her around the waist and set her down on his knee. "I'd like to share with you."

"Share with me?"

He pressed his fingertips to her jaw and turned her head. Then he kissed her. Long and deep. "Yes. I would like to share with you."

He swirled his fork around the pasta, and brought it up to her mouth. She opened without thinking, and took a bite.

Then he did the same, taking a bite for himself. It thrilled her. And she wasn't even quite sure why. Perhaps because this meticulous man with such a routine was being playful with her. Was giving her things that she was entirely certain he had never given to anybody else before.

It felt... It felt like a revelation.

And it made her tremble.

Because it felt dangerous.

Oh, so dangerous.

"I should get my own plate," she said, wiggling away from him.

"I don't like it when you're demanding."

"Well, that's too bad. Because on Wednesdays, I feel I might be very demanding."

"Wednesdays?"

He looked like he was considering whether or not he should make a note in his calendar. *Polly will be demanding. Recurring event.*

"Or Thursdays. I'm unknowable."

"You are not."

"I'm not?" She sat down at the table, her heart pounding a little bit harder than it needed to be.

"No. You are very knowable, Polly. You like summer and sunsets, and cake. You keep chocolate in your purse. Half the movies you watch make you cry."

"Those first few things are not unique, and also how do you know that about the movies?"

"I've overheard you telling a great many of your coworkers about a movie you have seen over the weekend, and about half the time you say that it made you cry. You are very soft, but at the same time you are very strong. I do know you."

"Oh."

"Tell me. About your parents."

"I did."

"You gave me a general idea for why they were a problem. And I want to know. Specifically. My father did not want me to be the person that I was. He wanted me to be the person he wanted me to be. And that I think is a terrible thing for a father. My mother loved me exactly as I was, and even then losing her, she helped me find myself. That is what a good parent does. Even when they aren't there, the love that they gave you does its good work. And so I want to know. What did your parents do that is so terrible that you left Indiana—"

"A lot of people leave Indiana."

"What did they do that was so terrible that it makes you not want to return home? I assume you don't wish them to even know you're having a child."

"I can try to explain it to you," she said. "But I'm afraid you'll just…" Suddenly, awfully, she found herself getting weepy. It was the pregnancy hormones. And him. Maybe just somebody else asking about her life. About her. "You can't just put me on the spot like this, Luca. I have perfected my mask."

"You haven't. I had the right of you from the moment you first walked in here. I knew that you were not half so sophisticated as you pretended to be. I knew that you were overawed to be in a company that size. I knew that it wasn't the blasé thing that you were trying to pretend that it was."

"Well. You are insightful."

Her chest felt tight.

"Tell me," he said.

"I have told people. I told the guidance counselor at my school when I was in high school, and he just said it was normal to have conflict with your parents." She blinked back tears. "It's so hard to explain. Because it's like I was responsible. For being an emotional barometer. I had to read the situation around me and react accordingly. And if I didn't, then I was going to have to deal with the consequences. Because it wasn't so straightforward as my father walking around acting angry. He would seem fine. And in fact, he would bait me into conversations that would end with him screaming at me. Because he wanted a fight. And so he would manipulate me until he got one. And my mother... She wanted me to be obedient. Biddable. And the way you accomplish that is by making sure that someone doesn't have a sense of themselves. Of their worth. She was an expert at making me question myself. If I would tell her about something that happened at school she would ask me if I was sure that that's what happened. Somebody hurt my feelings she would say... Maybe that isn't how it went. Maybe you were the one in the wrong. Before I would leave for school she would say, did you think that looked good?" She shook her head. "It was just such a perfect storm. But they didn't beat me. They didn't starve me. They just made me feel like everything around me was unstable. Like I had to walk on my tiptoes to avoid causing an avalanche. That was all."

But it had been so heavy. And carrying it all this time had been a weight she hadn't known was still resting on her shoulders.

"That would have been my undoing. I already question everything that I do, and often have to question my interactions with people. If somebody sought to undermine me in that way, it would've broken me."

"You're the smartest man in the world."

"That wouldn't have made me immune to the sort of gaslighting you're talking about experiencing." She loved how he didn't protest the label. "It is incredibly damaging. When you feel as if you cannot trust your own perception."

Her heart twisted. "You feel like that a lot, don't you?"

"Yes. And so I take refuge in the things that I can know. The things that I can learn and memorize. Because when it comes to those things, I am vastly superior to the people around me."

He was gently teasing. Except he also meant it.

"You are. You definitely are."

"I'm sorry. Do you… Do you feel as if I'm unpredictable? I know that sometimes the things that I want don't make sense to the people around me, and that must feel unpredictable."

"It did at first. But eventually I learned exactly what you wanted. You're actually very good at saying what you want. Nobody has to guess. It isn't a game that you're playing. I find that extraordinarily comforting. Given the way that I grew up. Given the way that my parents excelled at making their moods into a guessing game that I was forced to participate in. And… I'm trying to figure out how to say this. But the things that you need, the details. The details that you had me in charge of that you say you don't want to be bothered with, when in fact they are so important because if they aren't dealt with…"

"Nothing works for me."

"Exactly. They are not separate to you. They are part of you. And they are not a burden."

"Thank you. Though I will be working at changing how I regulate those things."

"Alternatively, you're a billionaire, and you could hire about six people to see to those things."

"Yes. I can. But the problem is… I became very dependent on you. And when you left, I thought that everything felt wrong because I needed you there to manage me. To manage all of the…the peculiarities. But it was more than that, and I couldn't see it. Also I… I suppose I cannot depend quite so much on one person for that sort of thing."

"There's nothing wrong with that." She moved toward him. "Nothing wrong with wanting to be more self-sufficient. But as far as I'm aware, that is part of having a partner. You figure out how to do things for each other. How to help each other. How to serve each other." She went to the center of the table and took hold of her gift bag. "Here. Open this."

He looked at the bag, and then up at her. "All right."

He took hold of the bag, and she watched, her breath frozen in her lungs as he began to pull the paper away, as he reached inside and took out the little red car.

His face was blank. She couldn't read it. She had no idea if he was happy, or if he was upset. If she had crossed some kind of line.

"Do you… Do you like it?"

He looked up at her, something fearsome in the depths of his gaze. "You know, I have never liked opening presents in front of people."

"Why not?"

"Because I know my reaction is not what people are looking for."

"I'm not upset by your reaction. I just want to know if you like it."

He smiled then. Slowly.

"Of course I do. It is…incredibly thoughtful. I don't think anyone has known me since my mother. But you do. You listened to me. You… You're right. That is what our partnership can be."

It still somehow felt like not quite what she was reaching for, but she didn't want to define the ache inside of herself.

She didn't want to have anything to do with it.

Because it was too much. All of this.

The intensity of the feelings that had held her in their grip since…

Since she had first met him.

It really would be a terrible thing to love him.

But she wasn't sure if she had the resources left to fight against it. Not anymore.

She stood, her heart thundering hard. Then she walked over to where he sat, and put her hand on his chest. "Luca."

He reached up, and pulled her head down, kissing her. Consuming her. And when they pulled away, there was something like wonder in his eyes. "I really love this gift that you gave me. But I don't lose everything when I look at it. Only when I look at you."

It meant something to him to say that. To feel that. She might not know entirely what, but she could hold close that it did.

She kissed him, holding his face in her hands as she did. Cradling him. Because he was precious.

Oh, no.

She was familiar with lust, protectiveness.

But this was something different.

This was something more.

He was such a brilliant man. Such a beautiful, brilliant man. And really, what other man on the face of the earth would she rather have as the father of her baby?

He was strong and determined. He… He loved. With so much of himself. His mother's death had taken that love and turned it into something he was trying to give the world. Everything he did was care.

Of course he would be the most wonderful father.

"You are amazing," she whispered against his mouth. "And I'm so sorry that I doubted what manner of father you would be. There is no other man I would rather have as the father of my child."

He growled then. And he lifted her up onto his lap, onto the dining chair. Her thighs were on either side of his waist, and she could feel his growing arousal there between her legs.

They kissed, and he held her close. Tight. Like she was the one who was precious.

No one had ever treated her that way. But he did. Imperfectly, perhaps, but she wasn't perfect with him either.

She was sometimes petty, and often selfish. She possessed far too great an ability to take the things he did and make herself feel persecuted because of them when there were moments she just had to accept his behavior wasn't about her, and she didn't *need* to make it about her.

It was easy for her to think that because some of the things he did were different than ways other men behaved, that he was somehow the project, but the truth was, she didn't know how to blend her life with another person's. She didn't know how to see grandly beyond her own perspective.

She was no less work. And perhaps she was more, because he had spent his life taking fearless inventory of himself, because he had been forced to. Because the people around him had always been harsh and uncompromising in their appraisal of him. Because people had treated him as if he didn't have feelings, which meant the way that their approach to him was often bracing.

Yes, she had been badly treated. By people who had wanted to treat her badly. Her parents had been difficult. They had been undeniably cruel in many ways. They had done nothing under the guise of care, and it seemed to her that often throughout Luca's life people had said horrendous things to him under the guise of helping him. Under the guise of forcing him to behave in a way that made them more comfortable. Not in a way that might make him more comfortable.

She committed herself then and there to being different. To handling him with greater care.

She kissed him to show him that.

And he kissed her back, physically demonstrating to her that she mattered too.

They could do this. They could make this partnership. They could have this life.

She felt a renewed sense of purpose. A sense of joy.

Luca wasn't her job.

He was her choice.

And she wanted to show him that.

She moved from his lap, and took his hand. "Come," she said, smiling.

"I'm not a dog," he said. "You can't give me commands."

"I think you'll find I can if you want to follow them," she said.

And he did, because he went with her into his bedroom.

She moved to him, beginning to unbutton his shirt, revealing the hard planes of his chest. The glorious acres of muscle that his clothes spent all day hiding—a real tragedy in her opinion.

She divested him of his shirt, kissing the hollow of his throat, his chest.

"I think you'll find yourself much happier if you take orders from me."

And that was how she found herself lifted up off the ground and deposited to the center of his bed. She watched with hungry eyes as he took off the rest of his clothes, and then moved to the bed, a glorious predator in his natural habitat.

There was nothing uncertain about him here.

Of course, there was nothing uncertain about him in most areas of his life. It was only that the last bit of time had thrown him into something he had never dealt with before.

And she was witnessing firsthand how difficult that could be for him.

But this… Oh, no, in this he was a master. And that was clear.

He moved his hands over her clothed body, slowly. Achingly so. She felt like she was going to jump out of her skin.

She was alive with need. And it went somewhere beyond simple desire. Not that desire had ever been simple with him.

It had been bound up in restraint. The restraint of knowing she couldn't act on it because she was his assistant. And knowing that even once she had she had to keep parts of herself back to avoid getting hurt.

What if she didn't.

What if, for the first time in her whole life, she was honest with another person.

She was honest with herself.

What if she gave everything?

Absolutely everything.

What would happen then?

And she felt all the resistance inside herself beginning to fall away.

She felt as if a light shone down upon her.

Radiant. Honest.

She felt as if she was seeing herself for the very first time.

And she wanted him to see her too.

He kissed her neck, and undid the buttons on her dress, slowly peeling the thin fabric away from her body.

He took off her bra, kissed his way down her stomach to the center of her thighs. He fastened his mouth to her over the lace panties that she wore, and she gripped him tightly.

He seemed to delight in the act of pleasuring her. Tasting her.

And she surrendered to it. He stripped her naked, his tongue sending her over the edge, his clever finger driving her mad.

And with each stroke there between her thighs, she felt her resistance fall away yet more.

Not a physical resistance. There had never been any physical resistance to him at all. But the emotional resistance.

It would be such a terrible thing to love him.

She did love him. She had. She had told herself that as a warning that came far too late.

Alarm bells that went off after the disaster had already occurred. But why was it a disaster?

She had learned to arm herself, protect herself, because caring about people who didn't care for you had been the hallmark of her life, and she had hated it. She had run from it.

But she couldn't let her parents define what she was capable of feeling forever.

She couldn't allow that to define her. To decide how happy she got to be.

Because it was all just fear. Fear that held her captive. Fear that manipulated her.

It was all it was.

She was allowing herself to be manipulated yet still. She didn't want it. Not anymore. She wanted to be herself.

She wanted to feel herself.

She wanted to feel him.

And when he traveled back up her body to claim her mouth in a searing kiss, it was everything. The taste of her own desire on his lips, the evidence of how much he cared about that. Of how much she was able to surrender when she was in his arms.

This was honest. It was raw, it was real. It was everything. That she wanted so badly for the two of them to be everything.

She wanted to find out everything she could be. Everything she could have.

And she felt closer to that than she ever had in her life.

When he thrust inside of her, it was like the sun had come out from behind the clouds. Blinding, brilliant and clear. And when he began to move, building a symphony of pleasure from deep within her, she surrendered.

It was so beautiful it was almost painful. It was so brilliant, she could barely look directly at it.

It was everything. So was he. So was she.

They were everything. And it didn't scare her.

Because Luca had never taken her feelings and used them against her. Because he had never sought to twist or manipulate what she felt.

He probably didn't even know he could. Because he probably didn't realize how much she cared.

They both suffered from the same thing. They had both been in a desert when it came to love.

She didn't want to be. Not anymore.

She kissed him, and he growled, lowering his head and biting her neck, making her gasp with pleasure.

She exulted in him. In his power, in his strength.

In the fact that there was safety in it.

Because he would never use it against her. He never had.

She could trust him. It was like a wave broke over her, warm and excruciating all at once. She could trust him not to manipulate her. He was safe.

When had another person ever felt safe?

Not ever.

He would never use his power against her.

Not the power of his mind, not his heart, not his body. He was exacting, and he was demanding, but there was always him right at the center of it.

And he was a very good man. That was what it came down to. Everything else they could learn to navigate. But he was good.

She had never known what it was like to love somebody who was good.

That realization broke her open, and when her orgasm struck her like a wave, it broke something inside of her. Then she began to weep. She clung to his shoulders, as she cried out his name.

Because she was all in on this. All in on him.

It was everything. So was he.

They were everything.

She clung to him. And then she whispered in his ear. "I love you."

CHAPTER THIRTEEN

HE PULLED AWAY from her, his dark gaze fierce. "I don't know that I can say that to you."

She wanted to weep. Not because she was heartbroken. Because he was everything she had believed him to be. "You don't need to. A dishonest man would say it to keep me happy. To keep me doing what he wanted. But you're not a dishonest man. That's why I know that I can love you. It's why… It's why it doesn't scare me. Well, that's a lie. And I want to be honest. It scares me, Luca. But I have been falling in love with you by inches all these years. When I left as your assistant, it wasn't because I found it difficult to keep up with your demands, even though I said that it was. Even though I wanted to believe that it was.

"I wanted to be singular to you. Not just an employee. And the fact that I might never be broke my heart in a deep and difficult way.

"I didn't want to admit it. So I made up stories. Because I'm very good at that. Because what I learned from my parents was how to twist reality when it didn't suit me. And even though it was used against me, I figured out a way to take that and make feelings and truths for myself that made me more comfortable. I want to be more like you. I want to see things as black and white. I want to see the heart of the matter. I feel like you do. I feel like the way that you deal with me and all the people around you is so… It's honest."

"You say that like it is a good thing. To have nothing nuanced to say about a situation, but I don't know that that's the case. I also have nowhere to hide. And sometimes I wish…"

"You have managed to hide though, haven't you? Because people don't get close."

"It is the only way for me to hide myself. Because as you can see, when you get close enough, you can see everything. Thank you for the car. I feel grateful for it. And deeply uncomfortable to have that part of myself so exposed."

"Why?"

"Because it is a vulnerability. And when people can hit you at your most vulnerable then…"

"I won't use it against you. I promise. I know that I did."

"It's all right. Because that moment was possibly the closest I came to trying to manipulate you. It might've been a clumsy manipulation, as you pointed out. I did not pretend to be doing something I wasn't. But I did use fear against you."

"And we both regret it. We can move on from it."

"Thank you."

"Are you terribly uncomfortable?"

"I'm not uncomfortable. But I find that I… I find this challenging."

"Why?"

"I can't put into words."

"And perhaps I find that most difficult of all. I am used to knowing everything. Everything in my sphere. I have built a life for myself that doesn't challenge these deficiencies in me. And here you are. Forcing me to work on every single thing I decided I didn't have to work on. I don't find it especially fun."

"Maybe it's not supposed to be fun. Changing. But sometimes it's necessary."

"Yes."

He looked at her. And there was something like wonder in his eyes. "Why do you love me?" The hunger there was something she couldn't deny, even as she felt a small wave of sadness wash over her. She wasn't going to demand that he suddenly feel the way that she did. She wasn't going to demand that he suddenly feel differently than he did.

But she wanted him to. Still, loving him had to mean loving all of him. And he was not going to turn on a dime. Not when there was clearly a block inside of him where the idea of love was concerned. Not with her child, it didn't seem, because he was able to see clearly the ways in which his father failed him, and he wanted to combat that.

But in every other way, it seemed to be very difficult.

"You are somebody who took great tragedy and turned it into purpose. Anyone would admire that." She cleared her throat. "But it's more than that. You are every inch yourself, and that makes me want to be the same. When I've spent my whole life hiding. Being with you has changed me. It's allowing me to get down to the truth of myself in a way that nothing else ever has. I don't feel afraid to be myself because you're yourself. I love your passion. Both from my body, and for medicine. For figuring out how to be the best father you can be. The way that you see yourself is so...unkind sometimes, Luca. And that makes me sad. But I'm also in awe of what it has allowed you to do. I can appreciate that, even while wishing you could be a little bit kinder to yourself. I love how you listened when I said you had to give care in a way that people could receive it. Even though I made you mad. Mostly, I love that I could trust you with all of this. I know that you won't take it and realize that you could crush me with it. Because that's not who you are. You're a brilliant man, and you could've taken all that brilliance and used it to exploit those weaker than yourself. You could've made money at the expense of other people, and instead you dedicated yourself to try and save others. That's incredible. It is something that most men with that capacity simply don't choose to do."

"Those don't seem like extraordinary things to me. They simply seem like the right thing to do."

"And it is your clarity on that which I also love."

She looked him in the eyes. "Don't devalue the things that you do simply because they seem clear to you. They don't seem clear to the rest of the world. And if they did, it would be a much better place. You are part of making it better. I love you for that also."

"I'm sorry. But this is much like opening a present, and not knowing quite how to react."

"You don't have to. You don't. Just be you. And that's enough. I promise you."

They were silent for a long time after that, and she felt her heart rate return to normal. Some of the adrenaline of the previous moment wearing off.

But it didn't feel finished.

It didn't feel over.

She was in love with him. And she wanted more. But she knew she had to let him get there in his own time.

And as she lay beside him with her hand on his chest, over his heart, she did her best to believe that it was all possible.

But Polly had never seen a future that contained love like this.

So she had a difficult time planning for it. A difficult time seeing how she might triumph.

But she had to trust. Because she had put her faith in this love rising up inside of her, and she needed to believe in it.

She needed to believe in them.

And as she listened to his breathing slow and his heart rate return to normal she held fast to that.

She had to believe in him.

She had to.

CHAPTER FOURTEEN

LUCA'S LIFE WAS entirely different than it had been three months ago, and he was…happy about it in many ways.

Polly had begun work at the company, dealing in marketing, and she seemed to thrive in that role. He liked watching her achieve things, accomplish her aims.

He liked her.

He loved having her living with him. He loved having her in his bed.

He enjoyed watching the changes that the pregnancy was making on her body.

This commonplace thing made miraculous because it was theirs.

Because she was his.

But she told him that she loved him nearly every day, and it was creating a dissonance inside him he was having difficulty ignoring.

It was beginning to build, like a low-level frequency that began to drive you mad.

How could it not. This… This declaration of love.

It was beginning to ring so loud in his ears that he couldn't hear anything else.

They went to another doctor appointment, and it was like something with claws had reached into his chest and speared his heart. Like it was being pulled asunder.

He couldn't seem to find any protection for it. And it was a monstrosity the likes of which he had never experienced before.

Nor did he want to.

And it was a terrible thing, because he wanted her in his life, he wanted to claim this thing that he was certain he could have, and yet, he was undone by the feeling that he was doing it wrong.

He was different. He could think he was doing the same things as other people and discover he wasn't, actually. He could think he knew what someone else needed and be wrong.

Wrong. Wrong. Wrong.

His father had always told him he was wrong.

His mother had told him he was right as he was, but she had died and he had no way of knowing if she would have always thought he was okay, or if she would have seen him struggle later and...

What if he was broken?

What if he would never be able to be there for her in the way that she needed?

He wanted to be.

She had told him that he needed to show care in the way that another person could receive it. The truth was, she had said she loved him. And that must mean on some level it was the sort of care she wanted shown back to her.

What did he know about that?

But even if so, it was like having somebody watch him open presents.

He wasn't sure if his response was acceptable. He wasn't sure if it could ever be.

He was sure of nothing.

Nothing at all.

What he wanted to do was engage in an exploration of his own soul. Come to some kind of medical conclusion, and yet that was the problem with humans.

Nothing was half so simple. Even when he wanted it to be.

He understood that for most people, medicine and medical science was the mystery. But to him…it was this.

And he had no way of knowing if this was just him, or if it was something that could be changed. Learned. If his mother had lived, would everything be different? Would he be…not a top medical scientist, not leading the field in research and development, not a billionaire, but a man. Who understood how to have a wife, who understood how to be a father.

Was it a lack of what he had been able to see and learn and experience that created these problems now?

All he knew was that he felt inadequate. Down to his very soul.

And for her part, she seemed happy. But what if she wasn't? And what if he could never know? What if she was simply putting on a brave face? Or what if she was blinded? Blinded by the love that she claimed to feel for him. Hadn't her parents kept her with them, kept her unhappy, likely because she was a child who had loved them?

He hated the idea of that. Truly.

And yet, she was…

She was the greatest thing in his life.

And also caused him the most unrest. The most pain.

She came into his office that day at three thirty in the afternoon. And he was stunned by her beauty. All over again.

Because everything was May twenty-fourth, over and over again. Because everything was her, trapped in the golden light of the sun. Because everything was them.

And he supposed it would always be that way. But he wondered if he had the capacity to make it something more than what it was now. To make it all the things that needed to be.

"Do you miss Milan?"

"No." She didn't look confused, and she did not ask follow-up questions. She just went about her business in his office as if it was hers. He supposed she knew where everything was in it. Knew it just as well as she knew him. Which was well.

"If you could go back, would you, though?"

She shook her head. "No. I had actually somewhat decided that I wasn't entirely happy with the job. It's difficult to go to any other job after you've been doing the work that we've been doing. Especially when I see the strides that you're making. It isn't that there isn't validity in something like fashion. Of course there is.

I really do believe that beauty and art make life worth living. But you make living possible. For so many people. And that work just feels so essential. It's difficult to leave it behind."

He nodded slowly. "Yes."

This office was sacred. Their working relationship was sacred. It was a rule. And yet, suddenly things did not feel neat inside of him. They felt like too much. Too big. And the gall of her saying she loved him sounded inside him over and over again.

He was overcome by it. Overwhelmed by it. He could hear nothing else.

And this was the thing he would always have a hard time explaining to other people.

Sometimes the noise inside of him was so great that the noise on the outside added to it was unbearable. That what was soft to them was overwhelming to him. That what felt like a breeze to them could become daggers beneath his skin, because the world within him was so overwhelming, so insistent, and he did not know how to share it with another person. Didn't know how to let anyone else know.

And he had tried with her. He was still trying.

But the way that he could most effectively communicate was through touch.

Not in the office. It was against the rules.

And then he found he could not hold himself back. She lived with him. Shared his bed with him. He had upended his routines for her. His life. And it somehow still didn't feel like enough. The unfairness of it all weighed down on him. Heavy and insistent and intense.

He wrapped his hand around the back of her neck, and he pulled her in for a kiss.

She gasped. Shock, but not displeasure. He knew her well enough to know that. He could trust that.

That, somewhere deep within him became a rallying cry.

He kissed her, and suddenly, it didn't seem to matter quite so much that everything was everything. That everything was overwhelmed. That everything was foreign.

Because she wasn't.

She was just the right amount. Just the perfect thing to take him out of his own head, and ground him in his body in a way that felt real. In a way that felt right.

So he kissed her, because it was the only thing that could quiet this noise inside of him.

She wrapped her arms around his neck, and kissed him back, and even though he hadn't said anything she seemed to understand. That he needed her. That he needed to demolish this last wall.

The sacred space of work.

Rules. What were any of his rules?

What did they mean? He didn't even know anymore.

He had lived his life by them, and they had only gotten him so far.

Yes, he had made all of these advancements in medicine. He had been part of so many wonderful things, but as a human being, as a man, he did not feel as if he understood anything new. Anything real.

Anything deeper.

But there was her.

And she made the life he'd built for himself feel inadequate. He had been certain that he'd built up a kingdom, he had accomplished great things. He had made all he did well so big that his inadequacies would seem like nothing, and yet.

There was her.

She made him feel like he had to find a different way to be. A different way to feel, to breathe. She made him feel like he needed to be new, so that he could have her.

Her.

He had her now. She was his wife.

Dammit all, she was his wife. Not his assistant. She couldn't simply quit. She was having his baby.

And he needed her.

And so he kissed her. Lifted her up and set her down on the edge of his desk.

And then, in a wild fury, he stepped away from her, went to his door and locked it securely. Her eyes widened.

"I need you," he said.

"Okay," she said.

He wanted her to say that she needed him too, but hadn't she already said the most?

Hadn't she already said that she loved him?

"Tell me," he said. "Tell me that you need me too." It wasn't fair. He needed it all the same.

"Of course I need you," she said.

He was… He could see through her eyes. How little he made sense. Asking her if she wished that she could leave, and then locking the door, putting her up on the edge of the desk. Demanding that she tell him how much she needed him. Of course. He made no sense at all.

Not even to himself.

But he couldn't stop himself now.

So he claimed her mouth again, and again. Stood between her thighs and pushed her skirt further and further up her legs. He pressed his hand to her slick flesh, teased her until she was gasping with pleasure. Until she cried out for more. More of his touch, more of him.

And he gave it to her.

He undid his belt, the closure on his pants, and claimed her in one decisive thrust.

He hadn't believed her the first time she had told him that he had forgotten a condom.

Such foolishness now. He couldn't even imagine the man that he had been then. The one who had been so convinced he could never lose control.

A loss of control was life with Polly.

It was just life.

And so he took her. Over and over again. Letting himself feel everything.

The tight, hot clasp of her body. Her hot breath in his ear as her pleasure grew. As she began to whimper with need.

Yes. He needed her.

What if he always did? Like this.

What would be left of him?

He blotted that out. He gave himself over to his body.

To this radical feeling of being entirely in the moment. Of being entirely in himself.

He clung to her hips and held her fast as he thrust, hard and wild.

She clung to his shoulders, and cried out his name.

And he found himself falling. Tumbling over the edge into the abyss. His pleasure was all-consuming. But then suddenly, it was just Polly. A bright and brilliant sunrise that overtook his soul.

Her name was a prayer on his lips, and he shouted it into that sacred space of his office. Which was now no longer given to work. But given to her.

There were no longer any barriers left within him. And when he pulled away from her, to look into her eyes, the intensity of the pain that he felt was so absolutely overwhelming that he couldn't breathe.

"Polly," he said, his voice rough.

"Oh, Luca," she said, touching his face.

He pulled away from her. "I'm sorry."

"Don't be."

"But I lost control."

"Luca, you live every day of your life with such control I find that I enjoy being the thing that makes you lose it."

But he didn't. Yes, it felt good in the moment, but he found himself less and less able to claw back some of his agency. He found himself given entirely to the feelings that she created in him, and he couldn't simply come back to himself.

And if he couldn't do that, then he could maintain control. And if he couldn't maintain control…

He didn't even know who he was.

He pushed the dark thought away, and looked at her. At her wide eyes.

"I love you," she said.

It was like a knife blade wedged beneath his skin.

"No," he said. "I don't want you to love me."

"Why not?"

"Because it's impossible… It was impossible for me to give you what you want. It is impossible for me to care for you in the way that you need to be cared for."

The words were like flame, migrating up his throat, making him feel useless. Worthless.

He hated himself in that moment. More than anything.

He hated himself.

But it was true. It wasn't fair, if he could never love her in the way that she needed to be loved in order to feel it.

If he could never care in the way that it would matter to her. He had strong-armed her into marriage. And she felt things for him that…no one else had ever claimed to feel.

She felt things for him that he hadn't imagined anyone could.

And what fool was he but he could not return it in equal measure.

He ignored the burning pain at the center of his chest. He ignored everything. Everything but this one clear truth. He would take her. He would use her, as he had done when she was his assistant, and in the end it would be no different. She would leave him. She would be wise to do so.

When he was not able to give what she needed him to give, when he could not make her feel what she wanted to feel.

When every moment of their lives was her giving him the most wonderful, thoughtful present imaginable, but she couldn't look at him and understand the way that he felt. And he couldn't find the words to tell her.

He would fail her.

As he had failed to be the son that his father wanted.

He had perhaps lied to himself. That he could become the father his own child would need.

He had a purpose. That purpose was medicine.

It was clear. It was clear. He knew exactly what to do with the human body, but the mysteries of the human soul were beyond him. His own most of all.

How could he have thought to bring her into this mess?

It was wrong.

He had to let her go.

He had to.

"Polly, we cannot continue on like this."

"What are you saying?"

"I will never be able to feel the things that you want me to. I will never be able to show you the sort of care that you want, and I fear that it will be the same with our child."

"Have I expressed disappointment in what you have given me?"

"No. Sometimes."

"And when I have, I have asked for clear change, haven't I?"

"Yes, you have. But... With this revelation of love and my inability to return it..."

"Have I asked you to? Have I told you that it is unbearable for me? Have I told you that I need you to say the words back to me right now?"

"No. But you will. You will, and there will come a time when I have to figure out how to be this thing for you, and I don't know how. I don't want to spend half a lifetime failing you until you get to the point where you have no choice but to leave."

"Luca, what have I ever done to give you the idea that would happen."

"You quit the job. And whatever you say, you quit it because of me. Because of how I made you feel. Someday that will be true in our marriage. Someday... Someday you will do with me what you had to do with your parents. You had to walk away because they did not love you in the way that you needed to be loved."

"You don't trust me."

"I do trust you. That is the problem. That choice, it would be the right choice. It would be the correct decision. And I would not be a good man—I would not be the good man that you have said you know me to be if

I didn't…if I didn't take the first step in letting you go. Rather than wasting your time."

"You promised me," she said. "You promised me that you wouldn't manipulate me. You promised me that you would be there for me."

"I'm trying. With all of the limitations of my soul, I am trying. But I do not want to be the villain in this story."

"It seems to me you don't want to try to be the hero either."

"You don't understand."

"I do understand. I understand how difficult it is to open yourself up, to try to…clear away all the debris that gets stocked up inside of us because of life. Because of the ways that other people have hurt us, because of the way they make us feel about ourselves. I understand. I understand that this is you, being trapped in the pain that you've experienced, and maybe even pain you feel you've caused. But if you care about me at all, then listen to me. Believe me. When I tell you that I am willing to be in this marriage as long as it takes for you—"

"As long as it takes for me to learn how to love you," he said. "Come now, Polly. Do not play these games. You have no intention of being in a marriage where you're not loved. You want me to change. You need me to change."

"You need you to change," she exploded. "Because you want this. I know you do. You want to be a good husband, and a good father."

"I can't do it," he roared. "Because… Because it never

stops echoing in my head, because I can't make it stop. Because I'm trying to do my job, and it's you. It's only you. And the things that you said to me, and the way that it makes me feel when I look at you, and I cannot turn it off. It's with me all the time. All the damned time, Polly. And I cannot… I don't know how to be this way. I don't want to be this way. I want to be myself, however incomplete that is."

"Who told you that you were incomplete."

"You know who did. Do you want to know what happened to my cars after my mother died?" He suddenly felt charred. Hollow. He was going to give her this memory. But she wouldn't understand why it was so terrible. Except… She had told him. About the things her parents had done to her, and how nobody had listened.

"He packed them all up in big black garbage bags. And he took them away. He said that my preoccupations, my obsessions were not healthy. My mother was gone, and then my cars were gone. And I had nothing. Nothing to hang on to. I knew everything about them. And they were… They were like a point on a map to me. A way for me to see my place in the world, and I understand that they were toys. I understand that it shouldn't have eroded something inside of me, not the way that my mother's death did. But it was like my world wasn't safe. It was like I could trust nothing. And all I could do was cover my ears and cover my head, and lay on the floor and scream. And I didn't know how to come back from it. I hate…that feeling. I hate caring like that.

And I can't ever do that again. I can never be that boy who lost everything. Ever."

She reached out and put her hand on his arm. "You aren't afraid for me. You're afraid for yourself. And that is why I want different for you. It's why I want better. Because you remember the loss so severely. But what about the love?"

She righted her clothes, and moved away from him.

"What are you doing?"

"I'm leaving. For however long you need me to. You are right. It is a good idea for us to exist in the middle. It would be best if we…figure this out all the way. I'm so sorry that those things happened to you."

"Aren't you going to tell me they don't matter?"

"No. They do. But I'm asking you to try and care anyway. I'm asking you to try to love anyway. Not because I don't think those things wounded you. But because I know they did. Because I think we both deserve more. And better."

She didn't shed a tear. She didn't cry or beg. He knew that she wanted to. Because he had always seen beneath her mask. But instead she smiled, a sad smile. A constellation of happy and sad. Layers. Complexity.

And then she walked out of his office and closed the door behind her.

And something threatened to break apart inside of him. Something threatened to put him right back on the ground where he had just said he never wanted to go. So he took a breath, but he thought of his purpose.

He thought about medicine. And how his life had

been complete before Polly Prescott had walked into his life and shown him he might be missing something.

He would think about what was next. He wouldn't think about her. His life had been just fine before.

And it would be just fine again.

He would see to that.

CHAPTER FIFTEEN

Polly went to a hotel, because she had to believe that he would come to his senses. He would find her, she wasn't worried about that. He was resourceful. She wasn't exactly trying to cover her tracks.

But as the days passed, she genuinely began to worry.

That she had perhaps overplayed her hand strongly.

That she had perhaps overestimated the connection between them.

Though she hadn't.

She knew that he cared about her. More than that, he loved her, or he had the potential to.

But it scared him.

Her heart broke for the boy that he had been. And it broke for herself.

Because she was still being strong. She didn't know how to be anything else. She had tried. She had put herself out there. She hadn't managed his feelings. And look where it had gotten her.

She had thought that it was growth, and that growth would bring happiness. But she wasn't happy now.

She lay in bed, a king. She ordered room service.

She went to work virtually. Because she did still have a job. A job that she loved.

Anyway, he was still her husband, so it wasn't like they were broken up entirely.

She wanted to ask him what he thought was going to happen. Because they were still having a baby whether he wanted to be with her or not, and the way it had all dissolved...

Surely he wasn't thinking that he wouldn't be part of their child's life?

Poor Luca.

He wasn't a liar. Or a manipulator. All the things he had said he really believed. That he might not be enough for her. That he might hurt her.

But she also knew he was genuinely mostly afraid of being hurt himself. How could she blame him?

His father had been cruel. Outrageously so.

She couldn't be wholly angry at him for his inability to let that go instantaneously.

But he was right. She believed on some level that he would love her. Someday. And he had tried to tell her that wasn't the case.

Like it was a kindness.

"I still don't believe you," she said, mostly for her own benefit. Mostly for her own heart.

"I still love you."

And that, she did believe. Even though it made her cry so hard she could barely breathe.

He was trying to work. And he couldn't. And it infuriated him. He needed to keep everything separate.

This was what he was good at. This was his purpose. His mission. This was what mattered.

And yet… She was in everything.

She was even in his motivation to do work. Because medical discoveries made the world a safer place for her too. And he could so easily recall the terror he had felt when he thought that she was sick.

Lately, his research brain had been thinking about maternal mortality rates around the world.

He had been thinking about complications and pregnancy, childbirth. Ways that they might be mitigated. Tests that could be implemented.

His focus was split.

His heart was…

He gritted his teeth. He couldn't compartmentalize. That he needed to. He felt like…like he imagined other people must feel, except he was certain it was stronger. More powerful. Nobody could truly understand the way that he felt.

Not even Polly, for all that she showed him sympathy. What did she know. What did she know about him. Even if she gave him sympathy, she didn't really understand.

And when did that become a good thing to you? This idea that you can't be understood.

Protection. The word whispered across his mind. The landscape of all that he was.

For all the good it had done him.

He could feel her. Even now. She occupied him. She obsessed him.

He…

Suddenly, that temporary sealant he had managed to get over the crack inside of him began to burst.

He loved her.

The realization was harsh. Swift. And that was the gong.

Not her love for him resonating inside of her, but his own. But he was afraid to speak, afraid to acknowledge. Afraid to know.

He loved her.

He loved her, and he wanted her. He wanted her to love him. But if he failed her and she left then he...he would be reduced to nothing yet again.

And it would be worse, so much worse than anything else he had ever endured.

Why did people want this? Why did they write endless songs about it? Why did they...luxuriate in the glory of this feeling that felt like dying?

He loved her.

He loved her, and he wanted her to stay with him forever, she wanted to have this baby, and more besides.

He wanted a life where he could love more than one thing.

He wanted everything.

He wanted to be there for his child, no matter who that child was. No matter how they thought and felt. He wanted to change himself in his own perceptions to meet them where they were.

And he wanted to do the same for Polly. What he had been trying to do was control everything. Yes, he had done a great many things to try and give her what she wanted, but only within the bonds of control. When that control began to slip, when she was more consuming than the day-to-day work, or the rules that he had set out for himself, he had run.

He had run. Because what he felt for her was bigger than anything else that had ever existed inside of him.

And he had to go to her. He had no choice.

He had to.

Because what was the alternative?

He knew this life. It had sustained him for a very long time.

But something she had said had hooked into him. Into the truth of it all.

She wouldn't accept half because she wanted him to have everything.

And he wanted to know.

He wanted to know what that was like. And he wanted her.

There was no pain on this earth that was so strong it was worth hiding away from her.

All he had to do was surrender.

And there was nothing on earth more difficult than that.

But Polly was worth it.

Polly was waiting for room service. So when there was a knock on her hotel room door she got out of bed and opened it without checking.

And froze. It was Luca.

With the wild look that he had in his eyes in Milan. And somehow right then she saw the truth of it all. From the beginning.

"Luca," she whispered.

"Don't speak," he said. "I need to. I love you. I love you, and I am very sorry that I couldn't admit that before. I'm sorry that when I began to feel it, really feel it, what I did was run away. I made excuses. And I was right. I was. Because I could not have loved you in the way that you loved me if I hadn't stared down the fear inside of myself. And fear is all it is. I have been afraid. Afraid of what it would be like to lose you. Of what it would be like if I loved you with everything I was, and lost you anyway."

"Luca," she said, her heart twisting. "I can't believe that I ever thought you didn't have feelings. Because I began to realize that you love everything. Everything that you have done since losing your mother is you putting love out into the world. Rather than keeping it to yourself, rather than hiding it. You are one of the most generous, good men to ever exist. And certainly the best one I've ever known. And I'm okay with this not being perfect. I'm okay with it taking work. For both of us. Because I have never been more free in my life than I am when I'm with you. I have never been happier. I've never been more myself."

"It's the same for me," he said. "I have always been made to feel ashamed about…"

"Right. Even I've said things. Things I shouldn't have."

"I deserved it."

"No. Nobody should ever be made to feel like who

they are is a detriment. Who you are is a gift. And it's why I love you. Not in spite of. Because of."

"I feel the same. You… You bring a balance to my life I didn't know I needed. What I didn't think was especially possible."

"You don't really like it that much."

He chuckled. "I love you. That's enough."

She looked up at him, and she felt her heart swell.

She had been wrong. All this time. Being in love with him was the key to everything.

He was a wonderful man to love.

"You are amazing, Dr. Luca Salvatore."

"As are you, Polly Prescott."

Luca could definitely be a difficult boss. But he was the best husband. And over the years he proved that he was also the very best father.

To all six children that they had.

And when he was finally able to announce a definitive cure for the cancer that had killed his mother, all of the children were present to pay tribute to the grandmother they had never known, but the grandmother whose love had shaped their lives every day.

Because she had been Luca's reason. And that reason had led him not only to change the world, but to the most glorious, joy-filled life anyone had ever known.

And when each of the children presented him with a small car in front of a crowd of thousands, nobody understood why.

But Luca and Polly looked at each other and smiled.

Everything he had ever lost had been given back in greater multitudes than he could've ever imagined.

And the love between them was more powerful than anything else ever could be.

* * * * *

Were you captivated by Her Impossible Boss's Baby?
Then you're bound to enjoy
these other dazzling stories
by Millie Adams!

The Billionaire's Baby Negotiation
A Vow to Set the Virgin Free
The Billionaire's Accidental Legacy
The Christmas the Greek Claimed Her
The Forbidden Bride He Stole
Greek's Forbidden Temptation

Available now!

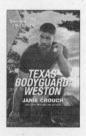